TED TAYLER

BARKING MAD

By Ted Tayler

The Freeman Files

Red Herring Season

Gathering Clouds

Still Standing

Vinci Books

vinci-books.com

Published by Vinci Books Ltd in 2025

1

Chapter One

Monday, 4 June 2018

GUS FREEMAN ARRIVED at the Old Police Station office a few minutes before nine o'clock. Was it possible so much had happened since last Monday morning? Where had those quiet, lazy days of retirement disappeared?

Seven days ago, he'd made the journey from his bungalow in Urchfont to the London Road HQ, looking forward to a new work week. But, instead, his Crime Review Team faced the prospect of a new case in which to immerse themselves. The mystery they were to grapple with was why on earth car dealer Dennis Gates died at the hands of a lone assassin back in September 2010.

Gus thought he'd spend the coming week searching for new witnesses, opening new lines of enquiry, and finding answers to the questions that remained after the initial investigation.

Today should have been the start of a second week on

the case that might bring those different threads to a satisfying, neat conclusion.

Those well-intentioned plans melted away within a minute of walking through the Wiltshire Police building's main doors. However, Gus could still hear Ricky Gardiner's chilling message, "Suzie Ferris dies if you open your mouth."

Within the hour, his superiors took decisive action.

Kenneth Truelove, the Assistant Chief Constable, agreed to block any attempt by the Chief Constable to interfere in the smooth running of the CRT. He would convince Her Majesty that nothing had changed. Work on the new cold case was the Crime Review Team's sole priority. The ACC would ensure Sandra Plunkett had no ammunition to use against Gus and his team.

Meanwhile, DS Geoff Mercer stepped away from his mainstream role, ostensibly due to a family emergency. Instead, he agreed to help Gus search for Suzie Ferris and gather evidence against the people behind her kidnapping.

As the lift took him to the first floor, Gus thought about how the past seven days had frazzled his team's nerves.

DS Alex Hardy was on gardening leave. The motorcycle pursuit rider had battled hard to return to work after a high-speed crash resulted in eighteen months of operations and recovery. Gus held Alex's reputation in high regard after the first two months they'd worked together. However, mistakes marred his work as the hunt for Suzie Ferris became more frantic.

Lydia Logan Barre suspected her lover used pills to mask the problems raised by accelerating the switch from wheelchair to crutches and finally from crutches to walking unaided. Gus had to face facts. Alex was unavailable until he conquered his demons. With Lydia's help, he would return to the fold in time.

So should DS Neil Davis. When things go wrong, they can go wrong big-time. No sooner had Neil resumed his place in the CRT office after his father's murder than his wife Melody suffered a miscarriage. Gus had no idea how traumatic an event a miscarriage could prove for the young couple, but he had enough sense to know Neil shouldn't rush. The team would welcome him back with open arms when he was ready to resume work.

As the lift doors opened, only two faces looked towards him. Lydia gave her usual smile. DS Luke Sherman nodded a silent greeting. These two then were the new, slim-line version of the Crime Review Team until further notice.

"Good morning, guv," said Lydia, "we're all set for the new case. Did you collect the murder file last Friday?"

"I did," said Gus, "and the ACC told me to forget it until today. I think the ACC believed we'd had a week packed with incidents, and it was only fair we took time to draw breath."

"We arrived two minutes before you, guv," said Luke. "The Freeman Files are up-to-date and can go to London Road once you've checked through them and added your contributions."

"Thanks, Luke," said Gus, "Leave that with me. You two can clear the decks ready for action on our next case. Please keep your fingers crossed we don't have any nasty surprises waiting for us. Last week provided us with more than enough."

"At least you had a quiet weekend, guv," said Lydia, "did you spend most of it tending to your allotment?"

"I squeezed in a visit," said Gus. He concentrated on the computer screen before him, hoping Lydia got the message he wanted to avoid further conversation regarding the weekend.

"Did you find out how DI Ferris is, guv?" asked Lydia.

Gus knew it wasn't an unreasonable question. Along with help from Geoff Mercer and WPC Amelia Cranston, his team helped bring Suzie home unharmed. Of course, everyone wanted to know how she was faring.

"We spoke over the weekend," he said. "Suzie is young, mentally strong, and although the doctors signed her off until the end of this week, it wouldn't surprise me if she made it into London Road earlier."

That seemed to satisfy the inquisitive young Scot. Gus glanced over the top of his monitor and saw Lydia wiping the first of the whiteboards.

Gus let the cursor on his computer hang for a while as he considered the quiet weekend Lydia believed he'd enjoyed.

Saturday morning was the first test of the new arrangement for Gus Freeman.

He'd woken at half-past seven to the sound of Suzie singing in the shower. She'd kept her word and allowed him to have a good night's sleep. Gus got out of bed and wandered in his boxer shorts to the kitchen. He needed sustenance. A bowl of cornflakes wasn't enough to set him up to move Vera Butler's furniture for a day. A proper cooked breakfast was in order. He started brewing the coffee.

"Good morning, sleepyhead," said Suzie.

Gus did a double-take at the youthful woman standing in the doorway.

A towel wrapped around her head was fair enough. The shirt that barely covered the essentials was the same one Vera donned the first time she stayed the night.

He had to agree it looked better on them than it ever did on him.

"I hope you don't mind," said Suzie, "it looked unloved hanging in your wardrobe, and my things are still in my car."

"I should have popped out to get your bag. I'm sorry."

"Don't go dressed like that. You'll get arrested."

"I was about to say the same to you."

"One of us needs to go," said Suzie. "Shall I cook breakfast while you shower and get dressed? It will be ready by the time you've done that and retrieved my things."

"What can I look forward to?" Gus had asked.

"As close to a full English as I can achieve with whatever's in that fridge of yours," said Suzie.

Gus had headed for the shower. This new arrangement was off to a promising start. Gus found no reason to change his opinion after they had eaten.

"That was scrumptious," said Suzie, "even if I say it myself."

"You're a woman of many talents," said Gus.

"I'm looking forward to riding out in the country," said Suzie, looking up at near-cloudless skies through the kitchen window.

"Can we squeeze another cup of coffee out of that percolator?" asked Gus.

"Half a cup each," said Suzie, "you can't put it off much longer. Vera needs you on duty by nine. After this coffee, it will be time to get into that car of yours and head into town. I must be off too."

They left the bungalow together at a quarter to nine and headed in opposite directions. Suzie headed for her stable in Worton. After dropping into the Community Shop for milk, Gus drove to London Road. He agreed with Vera that a quick walk to her new home was preferable to a forlorn search for a place to leave his car.

Gus parked in Geoff Mercer's bay and set off along the road. He was fifty yards from his destination when he heard someone calling his name. He recognised the voice.

"Morning, Mr Freeman."

"Good morning, Kassie," said Gus, turning to watch the young woman trot across the road carrying two heavy bags.

Some things never changed. Kassie's mop of hair now sported an orange streak, and the sleeveless top allowed her known tattoos to appear in public. Kassie wobbled to a halt next to him and caught her breath. Gus couldn't detect any added piercings.

"I've brought supplies," Kassie gasped.

"Have you been drafted in to help, too?" asked Gus, holding a hand to take one of her heavy bags.

"Thanks," said Kassie, handing over a bag, "yes, Vera asked me in the week if I was free."

"What on earth have you got in here, Kassie," he exclaimed, "it weighs a ton."

"I think I brought far too much grub. Vera's got the drinks covered, but workers can be greedy devils. I brought every type of baked goods I had in the house to be on the safe side. I can always take it back."

"I'll run you home afterwards," said Gus, "you could do yourself a mischief."

"Run me home?" asked Kassie. "Oh, it's true then. Vera said last week that you two weren't love's young dream these days. I thought you and Vera would christen her new home."

Gus gave Kassie a stern look.

"Vera and I are best friends, Kassie," said Gus, "I don't think either of us ever imagined it becoming more serious."

"Friends with benefits," said Kassie.

"None of your business, young lady," said Gus.

"All right for you," she said.

"Still no sign of your own Jon Snow then, Kassie?"

Kassie sighed.

"Perhaps, I should stop baking and find a hobby that isn't food-related."

"Here comes Vera," said Gus as her yellow Alfa Romeo turned the corner and parked at the end of the cul-de-sac.

A large removals van trundled into sight. Let the games begin.

"Hello, you two," said Vera, "sorry if you've been waiting long. The boys were late arriving."

"Kassie kept me company," said Gus.

Vera kissed him on the cheek and handed him another bag to carry.

"Everything we need to keep us in coffee or tea throughout the day's in there. Pop the milk in on top. There's just enough room."

Kassie was otherwise engaged. Her attention was on the removal men. Four well-built youths were preparing to unload the contents of the van.

Vera led the way to the front door. Gus followed her, hoping the handles of the bags lasted another ten strides. He heard Kassie puffing her way up the path behind him.

"Did you catch that testosterone, Mr Freeman? Today might not be a complete disaster."

Gus smiled. Hope springs eternal.

Six hours later, the move was complete, and the removals van returned to base.

Many of Kassie's buns got admired and devoured, and copious amounts of coffee were drunk. Vera was happy that nothing had got broken, and apart from a few minor adjustments after everyone had left, she could have everything where she planned.

"Thank you for today," said Vera, handing a glass of champagne to Gus and Kassie.

"What are friends for?" said Gus.

"I burp after I've drunk a sip or two of this," said Kassie, collapsing onto the nearest comfortable chair.

"Do you have to rush away, Gus?" asked Vera.

"Mr Freeman offered to give me a lift because of what I needed to carry," said Kassie. "Although with the grub those removals guys put away, I could manage on the bus. I'll need to bake again tomorrow to replenish my stocks."

"Yes," said Gus, "you wouldn't want to run out of supplies for Geoff Mercer's teatime snacks halfway through the week."

Kassie burped.

"Told you," she said.

"What about you, Gus?" asked Vera.

"I don't think I can compete with that, sorry."

Vera laughed.

"No, I mean, do you have to be somewhere?"

"Not for an hour or two," he said. "When Kassie's ready, I'll run her home to Worton."

"It's been a long day," said Vera. "I'll call my parents and persuade them to pop over later. I know my father wants to check he got good value for the money he paid that removals firm. After my parents leave, I reckon it will be an early night."

Kassie and Gus shared a look. He wondered whether Kassie expected him to return here as soon as he'd dropped her in the village.

"You chose well, Vera," said Gus, changing the subject and looking around the living room. "This place is a few minutes from work and next to the town centre. Moreover, it's compact enough to allow you to put your stamp on it without stretching the budget."

"It's ideal for one person," said Kassie, "it's the type of place I hope to get one day. You'll be happy here."

"Sure, I will," said Vera, "do you two want a coffee before you head home?"

"I couldn't drink another cup," said Gus.

"I'll risk another glass of bubbly," said Kassie, "and then we'll go home."

Thirty minutes later, Gus and Kassie made their way up London Road to the HQ's car park.

"Do I need to ask?" asked Kassie as she sat in the passenger seat with a bump.

"What?" asked Gus. "Where did I have to be in an hour? Suzie Ferris went riding today, and we loosely arranged that she would drop by the bungalow early this evening. We might grab a quick bite in the Lamb. Who knows?"

"Do you honestly believe that Vera's cool with how things have turned out?" asked Kassie.

"I stopped trying to work out how a woman's mind works a long time ago, Kassie," said Gus. "Whatever happens, I don't want anyone to get hurt, myself included."

Kassie was half-asleep before they reached the front of the old Rising Sun pub. Gus had to agree; it had been a long day. He pulled up and parked the Focus.

"Here we are, Kassie," he said, giving her a nudge.

"Enjoy your evening, Mr Freeman," she said, "do nothing I wouldn't like to do. See you on Monday, no doubt."

With that, Kassie grabbed her bags and headed for a gap in the hedge. Gus caught sight of a flash of orange hair behind the barrier and heard the house's front door, where she rented a room, slam shut.

Gus drove away from Worton and made for Urchfont. He checked his watch as he neared the bungalow; it was a quarter past five. If the driveway was empty, he could spare an hour to contemplate life on his allotment. There was no sign of Suzie yet.

The longer June days brought more sunshine and time to be gardening. Gus expected to see Bert Penman in his usual spot, but he found both patches of ground on either side of his allotment deserted.

It was Saturday, and Clemency Bentham had a busy day ahead. Perhaps this was the time she wrote her sermons. As for Bert, either he was in the Lamb, or he'd taken produce across to Irene North. There was plenty to choose from at present. Cabbage, cauliflower, and broad beans were ready to harvest now. Gus could see salad items that Irene might enjoy too. His lettuce, spring onion and radish plants looked ready to take to the table.

Gus studied his early potatoes and wondered how he had the cheek to call them his. Bert had done the lion's share of the work. Still, they needed lifting in a fortnight.

Gus decided he'd get on with the one job he could do without checking with Bert. He fetched his hoe from the shed. Almost from the first day he'd taken on this piece of land, Bert had told him to hoe at every opportunity to remove weeds and break up the soil. When the showers came, they would, before you knew it, allow water to soak into the earth. Gus passed the next hour, hoeing, thinning out and watering.

He did a little thinking on the new case too. It was only Saturday, and he'd promised to hold off until Monday, but old habits die hard.

Mark Malone's BMW had tinted windows, a lowered suspension, and a loud car stereo. He drove it at speed along the Beckhampton straight late at night back in 2015. That wasn't unusual. It was hard to resist speeding on that stretch of road. Hundreds of drivers got caught speeding there every year in the old days. Several died in high-speed accidents.

The Malone incident was different because he'd stopped at a JET garage on the A4 in Bath Road, outside Marlborough, fifteen minutes earlier. A grey 7-series BMW stopped behind him, and the two drivers appeared to argue. The attack might have been a case of road rage or mistaken identity.

As Malone reached the outskirts of Devizes, someone fired six shots with a handgun. Malone lost control of his car and hit several parked vehicles before ending up in a garden. He got hit twice in the head and died in the hospital later that morning.

Malone lived in Bath and had driven from a friend's house in Newbury. The original investigation, headed by Gus's old acquaintance DI Trefor Davies found nothing in Malone's background to suggest his involvement in any criminal activity. The detectives working the case thought the reason for Mark Malone's murder was linked to the events before the shooting. There was no evidence of any long-running dispute with anyone in the Devizes area. There was little to suggest a targeted attack. Nobody could have anticipated Malone driving in that spot at that time.

Gus tried to figure out whether Devizes had any direct connection to the murder. Was it little more than a convenient spot between Newbury and Bath that presented itself to the gunman?

So far, he hadn't studied the murder file in depth. How

did Malone earn a living? He was a week short of his thirtieth birthday when he died. The flashy car suggested Malone wasn't short of money, but that didn't always follow. Like many other young, thrusting entrepreneurs, he could have been living beyond his means. That was something to check on Monday when they faced this case.

As Gus cleaned his hoe before putting it back in his shed, another thought struck him.

Malone's friends lived in Newbury. Why not head for the M4 and give that BMW a treat? Malone wouldn't have been the first driver to press the pedal to the metal and cover the fifty miles in half an hour without getting caught.

Gus knew he shouldn't encourage drivers to break the law, but seventy miles per hour always felt too restricting on a motorway in perfect driving conditions. Moreover, the numbskulls who drove at fifty through a built-up area when children were going home from school irked him.

He was lucky if his Ford Focus could reach fifty miles per hour these days, especially between home and work. Nevertheless, Gus convinced himself it wasn't the car's performance that stopped him; it was the constant traffic volume.

As he drove along the lane towards his bungalow at a sedate twenty miles per hour, he filed away another question to add to Monday's list. Why did Mark Malone travel across the county via the old A4 road to reach Bath? A route where the opportunities to give the powerful BMW a chance to show its paces were few and far between?

As he turned into his driveway, Gus noticed that Suzie had beaten him to it. He parked beside her GTI, and she got out to greet him.

"Miss me?" she said.

"Hard to say," said Gus, "I've been so busy. I hope you

haven't been waiting long. Nobody was here when I returned from Vera's, so I popped along to the allotment."

"Don't worry. I only arrived two minutes ago. How did the move go?"

"It went smoothly," said Gus, "we had four willing men to do the heavy work from the firm Vera's father employed. Kassie Trotter came along to help. She supplied everyone with food and drink. Vera couldn't trust her with her breakable items; you know what Kassie's like. I dropped her off in the village with the few scraps that remained of her baked goods. She'll have a full day in her little kitchen tomorrow."

Suzie smiled.

"What?" asked Gus.

"Didn't you find it odd that Vera invited Kassie?"

"I hadn't thought about it until you mentioned it. Vera and Kassie work together every day. It makes sense that Kassie offered to help, doesn't it?"

"What was Vera doing this evening?"

"She invited her parents over to view her new abode," said Gus. "I think I see where this is heading now. Vera asked around mid-afternoon whether I needed to dash off anywhere. I said, not for two hours. Vera didn't press matters, and I didn't elaborate. The three of us then drank a glass of champagne to toast the new home, and when Kassie was ready to leave, we walked up London Road to retrieve my car from Geoff Mercer's parking spot. You think Vera had Kassie in attendance to avoid any uncomfortable moments?"

"It worked, didn't it? I assume Kassie came into town on the bus, and you're too much of a gentleman not to offer her a lift home afterwards. Vera knew that. It meant you could disappear with a valid reason and not worry about later because you knew her parents were keeping her company."

"You've got it worked out, haven't you?" said Gus heading for the front door.

"I wouldn't assume to have all the answers, Gus," said Suzie, "how are you feeling, anyway?"

"It's been a tiring day," he said as they stood in the hallway.

"Have a shower, freshen up and get changed," said Suzie, "I'll keep busy until you're ready, and then we'll go somewhere for a meal. Nothing too heavy. I'll drive if you wish."

"We could walk to the Lamb," Gus suggested.

"That sounds like a better idea. We can both have a drink then."

GUS BROKE into his reverie to finish his contributions to the Dennis Gates case in the Freeman Files. Lydia and Luke would soon wonder when he would start discussing their new cold case.

"Coffee, guv?" asked Lydia, noticing her boss was no longer staring at his computer screen.

"Perfect timing," said Gus, "I'm almost done with the Gates files. Next, I want to run through the bare bones of the Malone case and select items for the Hub to process. The murder file we've received from the ACC looks thin compared to the previous one."

"Mark Malone was only twenty-nine, guv," said Lydia, "it's no age, is it?"

"You can say that again," said Luke, "he was only eighteen months older than me. The same age as Nicky, almost to the day, when he died in 2015."

Lydia was on her way to the restroom when Gus's phone rang.

"Please don't let this be another Blue Monday," said Gus.

"Good morning, Freeman."

It was Kenneth Truelove, the ACC.

"Good morning, Sir," said Gus, "how can I help?"

"I need you and Geoff Mercer in my office at ten o'clock. Don't be late."

Gus was about to reply when he realised the ACC had ended the call.

"Trouble, guv?" asked Luke.

"The ACC didn't give much away, Luke, but I guess there's a balloon somewhere, and it's still rising. I'll finish this last paragraph, and then I can deliver the files to him in person. Let's hope that reduces his stress levels."

Five minutes later, Lydia returned from the restroom with three cups of coffee to find Gus preparing to leave.

"Was it something I said, guv," she asked.

"Trouble brewing," said Luke, "Gus got the dreaded Monday morning call."

"What on earth has happened now?" sighed Lydia as her boss disappeared behind the lift door.

Gus reached the ground floor and exited the building. He threw his files onto the passenger seat and clipped on his seat belt. Here we go again. As Gus eased the Focus into traffic on the High Street, he resumed his thoughts of the weekend.

Saturday night was the first time he'd visited the Lamb with Suzie. He and Vera always went further afield, sometimes to places neither was well known. Vera was still married at the start of their relationship, so it made sense.

Things eased in the last few weeks, but that changed last Sunday after his confession.

As Gus walked through the pub door with Suzie on his arm, he recalled that he and Tess rarely used the place. He'd been here with Neil Davis for Frank North's wake; it wasn't uncommon for him to have a quick pint with Bert Penman after a session at the allotment.

It was a different matter to arrive with a woman half his age. Several heads turned their way, and conversation stalled for minutes rather than seconds.

"We've caused a stir," said Suzie, "our secret's out."

They had enjoyed a drink and a bar meal while chatting over the day's events. It was very civilised, Gus thought. With each passing minute, the Lamb's regulars lost interest in them, and when Suzie suggested they leave at ten o'clock, Gus didn't think anyone noticed.

Sunday was a leisurely day. Neither of them was in a rush to get out of bed. There were no pressing appointments, so Gus decided it required brunch. He worked in the kitchen while Suzie showered and dressed. After they had eaten, Suzie suggested a walk in the fresh air. They left the bungalow at two o'clock, and she drove them to Westbury. She and Gus climbed the hill near Bratton to enjoy the view and consider the history of the White Horse carved into the chalky grassland five centuries earlier.

"Another Sunday, another journey back in time," said Gus, "it's amazing the number of places I've never visited in this county despite living here all my life."

"Modern life isn't everything it's cracked up to be," said Suzie, "I've always wanted to slow down, take time to look around me, rather than speed by in the car. That's the joy of riding like I did yesterday. It would be healthier for you, too, instead of sitting by your garden shed when you want to mull over a case."

"Look, young lady, I still bear the bruises from that trip I took on horseback to your farm. I'm too old to start riding, thank you very much."

"Don't worry, I won't try to change you," said Suzie. "I fell for the grumpy retired detective. Come on, let's get back. You can cook me something delicious, and then I'll leave you to catch up on your sleep."

Later that evening, after Suzie drove home to Worton, Gus sat in the lounge with a large glass of Malbec. He watched nonsense on TV for an hour and then headed for the bathroom. There were a few additions besides his shower and bathroom cabinet items. Well, it made sense if Suzie planned to stay over regularly.

This morning, when he opened the wardrobe door to grab his pale blue work shirt and dark trousers, he had another surprise. He found his clothes squeezed into the right-hand side, just like the old days when Tess allowed him to occupy a fifth of the available space.

Since her death, Gus had spread his few clothing items along the rail so it didn't feel empty. Instead, he thought back to yesterday. He and Suzie dressed casually, and he got a polo shirt out of a drawer with the same pair of dark slacks he'd worn on Saturday evening.

The extra clothing must have been put in the wardrobe since he got home from Vera's. Of course, that was what Suzie was doing when she kept busy while he showered after returning from Vera's.

Did this mean Suzie was moving in bit by bit? Or was it just enough things to survive a weekend? If he weren't due to meet Geoff and the ACC to learn of yet another crisis, he would need to give the matter thought.

How did he feel about what it might mean?

One thing Gus was sure of as he bounded up the stairs to the administration area.

How quickly things could change.

Geoff Mercer spotted him from the other side of the room. He waved a hand, and Gus waved back. Vera and Kassie were on the coffee round. They had plenty of doors to knock on before they reached the ACC's office. Geoff Mercer joined Gus outside the door.

"Any idea what's happened?" asked Gus.

"Everyone's tight-lipped this morning," said Geoff, "it feels serious. I hope it's news of Gardiner's arrest."

Geoff knocked, and the ACC called them in. He sat at his desk.

"There's no way to soften the blow of this news, I'm afraid," he said. "We received a call this morning from Staffordshire Police. As you know, the Chief Constable left early on Friday to spend the weekend in the Midlands. She joined her partner, Naomi Hall, at their home near Lichfield. Yesterday evening a dog walker heard an engine running but couldn't see a nearby car. She realised the sound was coming from the garage."

"Dear God, no," said Geoff.

"She called the emergency services, and they opened the garage door. But it was far too late to save the occupants of the car, Sandra Plunkett and Naomi Hall."

"Was there a note?" asked Geoff.

"A tear-stained envelope addressed to the Staffordshire Chief Constable was inside the house," said the ACC, "not much detail in the letter. Sandra apologised to her family and colleagues for a serious error of judgement in the past. No names, no pack drill."

"Sandra Plunkett couldn't face the imminent disclosure

of the facts surrounding the hit-and-run she covered up with Dominic Culverhouse," said Gus. "She realised her career was over. The shame was too much to bear."

"There was worse to come if the IOPC linked her to Terry Davis's murder," said Geoff Mercer. "They can't follow the money trail until Gardiner gets arrested, but if she and Culverhouse paid him to murder Terry as we believe, then a loss of career was the least of her worries."

"What have we done?" asked the ACC. He stood and walked to the window.

"Our jobs," said Gus Freeman.

DS Geoff Mercer nodded his agreement.

Chapter Two

IT WAS noon before Gus drove back to the Old Police Station office.

Geoff Mercer persuaded Gus to stay with Kenneth Truelove until Vera and Kassie delivered the coffee and biscuits. After they left the room, the two friends attempted to calm the ACC's nerves.

"We did nothing wrong," said Geoff, "Culverhouse and Plunkett did."

"The evidence we passed to the IOPC was damning," agreed Gus, "Culverhouse and Plunkett have nobody to blame but themselves."

"What about Naomi Hall?" asked the ACC, "she didn't deserve to die."

"We have no idea how much she knew of the incident six years ago," said Geoff. "Naomi Hall came from Oakley, and she and Sandra lived together for years. If she was innocent, could she merely walk away when her lover admitted what would happen? Perhaps, but how could we anticipate a double suicide would be the outcome?"

"Who knows about the deaths?" asked Gus.

"The Police and Crime Commissioner," said the ACC.

"I bet that woke him up," said Gus, "he'll wish he did something less stressful. That's two Chief Constables he's seen disappear since I returned to work."

Kenneth Truelove gave Gus a look that suggested he thought this was Gus's fault.

"Who's taking charge in the interim?" asked Geoff.

"Why do you think I'm getting stressed?" said the Acting Chief Constable. "All I asked for was a quiet rundown to retirement. No major crimes, scandals, or headaches; not much to ask after forty years of faithful service."

"Life's hard, and then you die," said Gus.

"That bloody Kierkegaard fellow again, I presume?"

"Sorry, Sir, he can't get the blame for that one."

"When are you going to announce this to the troops?" asked Geoff.

"The media people are getting a speech prepared," said the ACC. "The IOPC investigation is in its early stages, and they have yet to interview Culverhouse. Ricky Gardiner is still at large. The PCC hopes to finish this with as little fuss as possible. I can't see how, but that's the way he wants to play it. The only people outside this office who know the genuine reason behind the deaths are the Staffordshire Chief Constable and our Police and Crime Commissioner."

"So, you'll inform everyone working for Wiltshire Police and the local media that the Chief Constable and her partner died in a tragic accident," said Gus. "Or words to that effect. The hope is it will buy the IOPC time to nail Culverhouse and arrest Gardiner. Both events are forecasted to occur early this week, anyway."

"Yes, the truth behind the double suicide will surface in

time," said the ACC, "they'll delay the post-mortem as long as they can. For two to three days. We're very much relying on others to do what's necessary. We can only sit and wait, not the situation I prefer."

Gus had to agree with him.

There was a knock at the door. The Police and Crime Commissioner walked into the room. He glanced towards Gus and Geoff.

"Our regular Monday meeting with the head of the Crime Review Team," said the ACC. Gus closed his eyes. It might have been better to say nothing. Now the PCC will suspect we were discussing the hush-hush news.

The PCC nodded and handed over a draft copy of the speech for the briefing and press release.

"We should discuss this," he said to the ACC.

Geoff and Gus got up to leave. They knew when they were surplus to requirements.

As the door closed behind them, Kassie Trotter grabbed Gus's arm.

"What's going on, Mr Freeman?" she asked, "we knocked on Her Majesty's door and found it locked. Vera tells me her car's not in the car park. Her Majesty was out of sorts last Friday. She wasn't as bitchy as usual. As if she'd had enough, you know?"

"You'll hear soon enough, Kassie. Don't fret. How's Vera?"

"Her parents loved the house when they dropped in on Saturday night. She had lunch with them in town some-where yesterday. It doesn't seem right when you and Vera aren't talking about one another, Mr Freeman. I had such high hopes for you two."

"I understand that, Kassie," said Gus. "You can't force

these things. Did any of those four lads from Saturday ask for your number?"

"Each of them did during the day," said Kassie. "I haven't heard from any of them yet, though. Typical."

"They don't know what they're missing, Kassie," said Gus, "you've got a heart of gold. So before I finish this consultancy, lark, I hope to see you meet Mr Right."

"I live in hope," sighed Kassie. "DI Ferris returns to work on Wednesday, Mr Freeman. Although I expect you heard that?"

"I did not," said Gus.

"Half days at first," said Kassie, "then if she copes with the pressure, Mr Mercer said she could return full time from next Monday."

"Excellent news," said Gus as he dashed downstairs and left the building

IN THE CRT OFFICE, Lydia and Luke were at a loose end. They couldn't progress the Mark Malone case without instructions from Gus Freeman. Luke had prepared a search routine for the Hub to process. He imagined they might need a list of drivers charged with road rage incidents.

"Why do we need that?" asked Lydia, "it was only a theory put forward by the detectives in the original investigation."

"While road rage is not an offence in UK law, many incidents occur because of dangerous or careless driving," said Luke Sherman. "All reports, whether or not damage or injury has occurred, can get considered. There could also be criminal penalties for assault or more serious offences against the person."

Gus Freeman overheard Luke's explanation as he emerged from the lift.

"Offences against the person? That's public order offences, Luke, am I right?"

"Yes, guv. I wondered if we should get the Hub to interrogate the records for drivers whose actions on the highway might likely cause harassment, alarm, or distress. Then, we might have an extensive list when we add it to drivers who got nicked for driving without due care and attention around the time of the Malone murder."

"What else will you be asking from the Hub?" asked Gus.

"I scraped the bottom of the barrel to get that much, guv, to be truthful," said Luke, "did you have any suggestions?"

Gus blew out his cheeks in frustration and flopped into his chair.

"Would you like a fresh coffee, guv?" asked Lydia.

"No, thanks," said Gus. "The news I received from London Road wasn't pleasant."

"Can you share it with us, guv?" asked Luke.

"The Chief Constable died at the weekend, together with her partner. They don't suspect foul play. That's the statement the media will get."

"That's dreadful," gasped Lydia.

"We mustn't blame ourselves," said Gus. "It fully justified the work that members of this team did to highlight the criminal wrongdoings of others. As hard as it is, we must move on."

"That's something I can't always get my head around, guv," said Lydia. "I remember what you told us after you solved our first case. Our part in the process was complete. We'd analysed the evidence, questioned the witnesses, and identified Leonard Pemberton-Smythe as the killer. My natural reaction was to follow the story through to a senior politician's trial, conviction, and public shaming. A man who trumpeted family values and strong policing. You handed that part to DS Mercer and the Crown Prosecution Service without a backward look."

"The justice system isn't infallible, Lydia," said Gus, "but we have to rely on it finally getting the right result. That was the way I operated as a serving officer. When the ACC asked me if I wanted another chance to show how good a detective I was, I couldn't say no. I agreed to come back on the understanding that I could do just that; to detect. As for Sandra Plunkett and the others involved in the death of Terry Davis, we followed the evidence and established irrefutable links between the suspects and Neil's father's murder. Last week when our findings went to the IOPC, our job ended. In due course, I believed the guilty parties would face trial for whichever offences that evidence warranted. I made no recommendations; that's not for me to decide. I relied on the system to deliver the right result. The weekend events are tragic but irrelevant as they don't alter the facts. The Chief Constable covered up the death of Jason Whitworth in 2012 and then was complicit in ordering the murder of Terry Davis by Ricky Gardiner to continue that cover-up."

"Where does that leave us with Culverhouse and Gardiner, guv?" asked Luke Sherman.

"When I drove home on Friday, I must admit I hoped that by today Gardiner would be in custody. The IOPC could then carry out their investigations into our allegations. Do you have any idea of the scale of matters they cover?"

"I've heard rumours about the Met Police's ghost squad,

guv," said Luke, "they handle hundreds of accusations against our rotten apples, don't they?"

"There has always been a minority that sabotaged evidence or passed information to criminals and journalists in return for money. It's frightening to learn that others dealt with drugs and conspired to commit kidnap, violence, serious assaults, or even attempted murder. We have experienced instances of that in this office. The IOPC face a further problem when investigating a serving officer. They know what vehicles we use, our techniques and where to go, what to look for, and everything about how we operate. The people investigating Culverhouse and Plunkett would use their intelligence hub and surveillance teams so that no one else found out who they have under the microscope. They recognise that you never know who to trust."

"Did they issue a misconduct notice to Culverhouse and Plunkett, guv?" asked Luke.

"That is standard procedure, Luke. Whether the complaint came from a member of the public or an internal source, they should learn that they were under investigation. The ACC hasn't informed us whether either of them got served notice of suspension or restriction. If the Chief Constable got told on Friday, that might have triggered what followed. How Dominic Culverhouse reacted, who knows?"

"Watch this space then, guv," said Lydia.

"You know what my response will be, Lydia," said Gus, "it's out of our hands now. However, Mark Malone's death in 2015 is very much our case, and we must give it our full attention. So let's run through the bare bones of it once more to see what emerges."

Luke Sherman flicked through the murder file and read from a newspaper report.

"The shooting of a motorist is increasingly likely to be a

road-rage murder. DI Trefor Davies said yesterday they sought the owner of a grey BMW seen alongside Mark Malone's car only minutes before the shooting. The twenty-nine-year-old Malone's distinctive vehicle stopped next to the grey BMW at a JET garage outside Marlborough on the twelfth of May. DI Davies believed that the grey vehicle was crucial to the case. In addition, he thought the motive for the killing emanated from that period as opposed to past events."

"Did they even bother to delve deeper into the victim's background?" asked Lydia. "What did Malone do for a living?"

"He was a pet shop manager, returning to his home in Bath," said Luke. "Malone spent the evening with friends in Newbury."

"They must pay better wages than I thought for a pet shop manager," said Gus, "what does a BMW like that cost, Luke?"

"Don't look at me, guv. I couldn't afford one. You wouldn't get much change out of thirty grand for a customised model such as the car Malone drove."

"Why did DI Davies and his team raise the prospect of mistaken identity?" asked Lydia.

"It could have been a defence mechanism," said Gus, "a trap I've fallen into myself when younger and less experienced. A reporter might press you for an answer, or a relative can't understand why anyone would want to kill their son or brother. Malone's was a callous murder that left his family and friends devastated. People want answers, and they want them at once. The police need time to investigate every avenue, and that time isn't made available. So when a solution doesn't appear within a brief time, the detective team moves on to another case with a greater chance of success."

"I've found something relevant in the stuff they gathered, guv," said Luke. "The murder weapon was the catalyst for the mistaken identity theory. An innocent member of the public died during a turf war in Islington back in 2013. Mark Allison was a student at the London Metropolitan University. He died in a drive-by shooting late in the afternoon of October the twenty-first. Police believed the killer mistook Allison for a gangland rival. Allison's murder remains unsolved. When forensics collected evidence from the scene of Malone's murder, they confirmed that the gunman fired six shots. Two shots hit Malone, wounding him fatally, and he died in Swindon hospital around three hours after the shooting. The six bullets came from the same weapon. Ballistics proved it was the same gun used to kill Mark Allison."

"I don't suppose that will help," asked Lydia, "we can't just arrest the registered gun owner, can we?"

"It reduces the number of potential killers," said Luke. "We can start with that turf war in 2013 and identify the gangs involved. The Hub might match Mark Allison's photo to a known gang member to explain the confusion. That will indicate which gang carried out the killing but hit the wrong target."

"It's not our job to solve that murder, Luke," said Gus. "Who says the 2013 killer didn't toss the weapon straight after the shooting? That handgun could have had a dozen owners in the intervening eighteen months. As Lydia pointed out, it was an illegal weapon. We might find that Allison and Malone might pass for twins, and the 2015 attack was the killer finally getting his man. My gut tells me they're unrelated. Pass the enquiry onto the Hub if you wish, but make sure they understand it's a lower priority than a detailed list of Malone's phone records. I want to see his contact list, which of them he rang or messaged on the night he died, and where he found the extra money to afford a flashy motor. We have an awful lot more to learn about young Mark Malone."

Luke and Lydia could tell this case was shaping up to be just as difficult to solve as any previous cases they'd worked on together. Lydia wished Alex and Neil were back at work. Not because she didn't enjoy working with Luke but because she still considered the original line-up the A-Team.

They spent the rest of the afternoon digging into Mark Malone's background.

Gus Freeman left at five o'clock and drove to Urchfont. His first stop was the allotment. He unlocked the door to his garden shed and slid open the top drawer of an old wooden cabinet in the far corner. Underneath a pile of seed catalogues, he found the tobacco tin. Inside was an assortment of keys, none of them labelled. Gus knew which set was Tess's collection of house keys.

Gus had brought them from the bungalow after Tess died. You never knew when you might need a spare set. He had only an old shed door lock to replace if he lost his keys, not something costly at the bungalow.

The driveway was empty when he drove in from the lane—dinner for one this evening. So Gus kept the keys in his pocket until the right time, whenever that might be.

Tuesday, 5 June 2018

RICKY GARDINER WAS on the run.

That came from trusting other people. Two weeks ago, he had everything under control. The solicitors were handling the sale of his mother's properties in Cornwall and Birmingham. He could retire to the sun on the proceeds.

All he had to do was keep that good-looking copper in his mother's rundown old house in Leek Wootton for another couple of days. He hoped it never came to it, but for the right money, he would have killed her.

Another nice little earner, the same as getting rid of Terry Davis for his so-called partners. A piece of cake. When he returned to that dump they had the nerve to call a B&B, Davis was as drunk as a lord. He'd stood in the dark passageway and waited until Davis scrambled in his pockets for his keys. Ten seconds later, they were both outside on the fire escape. He stood at the top, and Terry Davis lay dead at the bottom. A quick dash down the staircase to check, and then he left Devizes on foot and got onto the Chippenham road.

When did things get complicated?

That phone call was when it went pear-shaped. Bad enough dealing with that low-life Culverhouse, but Plunkett always threatened to be a weak link.

Ricky didn't like women.

His mother never gave him the time of day. When he joined the Met and moved into a flat, it was the happiest he'd seen her. Did he ever give her any grief? Not really; he was never in trouble with the law at school. That took talent in the borough where he lived. Ricky wasn't a waster like his Dad, and he had a decent job as a copper, even if the pay wasn't brilliant. That's why he'd supplemented his earnings by helping a few people with information, turning a blind eye here and there, and losing bits of evidence. Every little helped.

The undercover gig brought more money and more opportunities. Ricky met many women in that game, but none interested him that way. So instead, he watched other blokes taken in by the bullshit they fed them. No chance; nobody dragged Ricky Gardiner around with a ring through the nose.

During that phone call, he listened to Sandra High and Mighty Plunkett getting squeamish about agreeing to get rid of Ferris. The young girl slept with Freeman, for heaven's sake. Of course, the kidnap was the perfect card to play; Culverhouse was right. Freeman ran around like a headless chicken, wondering where his lady friend had gone. His head was full of thoughts of a piece of skirt, not trying to end the careers of two high-flying coppers,

To make matters worse, Plunkett wasn't happy that Davis's death was not getting written off as an accident. Typical woman, always moaning. What did she want to do? Kid herself and her lover, it wasn't murder, so they carried on living in that house in the country with roses around the door? Culverhouse and Plunkett both wanted Davis out of the picture. No point bleating once he'd done the deed. Culverhouse turned on Plunkett and warned her there was no turning back. He should have acted sooner.

Ricky had wanted out at that point; he could see things falling apart. He had checked his bank account to confirm Plunkett had transferred the money for the Davis hit, and then he had abandoned the Ferris woman. Ricky cleared out as soon as he could and drove south. If he stayed in Leek Wootton, it was only asking for trouble.

Ricky hadn't worried about the girl. Someone would

find her, and Freeman would have her back home before she came to any harm. There was little evidence at Leek Wootton. He'd only used it as a convenient lock-up after Plunkett arranged for Ferris to attend some course or other. Kidnapping Ferris was too easy for words.

No, he was better off going it alone—no more partners.

Ricky was on home turf and knew Lewisham and Catford like the back of his hand. He ensured his hideouts were never near his father's place on Fordyce Road. The police were sure to watch that property.

As if he was stupid enough to go somewhere where his face was familiar.

When he reached London last Tuesday evening, his first job was to ditch the Audi at a breakers yard. He knew the right place where the owner owed him a favour. So Ricky slipped him a monkey to put a smile on his face. Five hundred quid on a quiet day will do that for many traders.

Ricky didn't need wheels to get around the city. He could travel anywhere he liked without anyone being the wiser. Twenty years undercover was a great training ground. If Plunkett cracked under pressure, Culverhouse would have to handle it. Ricky knew time was the commodity he needed. Just long enough to get the money for those property sales. There were papers to sign, things he couldn't do from Gran Canaria.

He'd needed time to think last Wednesday morning. He spent the night in an empty flat in Croydon. A place he'd rented for years when undercover. The Met knew of several cover identities he'd used over the years, but the sites he'd used, not so much.

It would take Freeman ages to untangle the various characters he'd assumed and where he'd lived under what name and background.

Nearly every place he'd rented across London was sublet now to someone who had no clue who his landlord was. Ricky was clever at covering his tracks. He'd planned for this eventuality.

Ricky paid the rent for the flats on the due date without fail. Then, after an undercover role ended, he advertised the flat in the nearest newspaper shop window. The monthly rental was always below the going rate. Every flat got snapped up within hours of the advert appearing in the window.

The only thing Ricky insisted on, apart from the happy client paying rent on time, was that they gave him a bed with no questions asked if he needed a place to sleep. Ricky had half a dozen hideouts to move to if the Croydon flat was rumbled. He left that flat with a backpack containing a few essentials. Spare clothes he'd stashed went in the bag along with the wash kit and toiletries he'd rescued from the Audi.

Since last Wednesday, he'd slept in Croydon, Pinner and Walthamstow. He'd moved around the city as little as possible, keeping a weather eye open for the law. The Met didn't cause him any headaches. Ricky knew their style. The ones you didn't know caused the problems.

The solicitors dragged their feet, as always. Only a matter of time, they said. That's what you said last week. Ricky shouted down the phone when he called them yesterday.

He felt the net closing. If only he knew who was hunting him.

How long after the police found Ferris did Freeman realise there was nothing to stop him from looking for Terry Davis's secret? That worried Ricky Gardiner.

He didn't call Plunkett on principle. He couldn't ask

Culverhouse for news; the swine didn't answer his calls. That burner phone they used to keep in contact must be in a skip somewhere by now.

Ricky preferred to work alone but being alone wasn't much fun when you didn't have anyone to tell you what was happening. So how could he determine whether Freeman knew more than Culverhouse thought about what happened near Oakley Hall in 2012?

Ricky sat in the Blythe Hill Tavern with a pint on the table in front of him. He had an unobstructed view of the door; everyone in the bar was a local. So he could relax for an hour while he thought.

When he followed the Ferris woman into the College car park on Friday morning, she'd talked to another copper. Did he have a photograph of her on his phone? He'd snapped several of Ferris that week. Ricky flicked through his phone. Yes, there she was, looking straight at him, sitting in the van.

If Ferris thought someone was following her, why didn't she take more care? She calls herself a copper. She fits right in with the current thinking. If you're female, gay or BAME, you're on a fast-track to the top, even quicker if you qualify on all three counts. It doesn't matter if you're a natural thief-taker like Freeman or a bloody good under-cover operator prepared to risk life and limb to nail a criminal. We're yesterday's men.

Ricky started the search on his smartphone. It took him eight minutes to find a name for the face. One good swallow would finish that pint, and he could get outside and give DI Josie Bennett a call.

Ricky Gardiner remembered a DS stationed at Snow Hill near retirement age. That was his first contact.

"Des, my old mate, how's things?"

"Who's that? Tony Fernandez, is that you? Blimey, you're a blast from the past," said Des Copson.

"Is Josie Bennett one of yours?" asked Ricky.

"She's here somewhere, mate. Do you want me to give her a shout?"

"Please, Des. Are you still watching the Villa?"

"No, mate, I stopped putting myself through the agony. After all, I realised they never came to see me when I was rough."

Ricky laughed. He'd heard the joke, but it paid to keep contacts like Des Copson sweet.

"Hello, who's speaking?" It was Josie Bennett.

"Josie, my name's Tony Fernandez, a mate of Des Copson's. I worked undercover on a joint operation with your lot with the Met back in the day. We're hunting a fugitive in my area. He's wanted for kidnapping."

"Oh, you mean the guy who took DI Ferris. I was with her that day."

"She's OK now, I hope?" asked Ricky.

"She's fine. Not back to work yet, though. I gave her a ring at the weekend. Just to catch up."

"Funny business, that kidnapping," said Ricky, "I can't work out the motive behind it. He never touched her, there was no ransom demand, and then he just disappeared, leaving her alone."

"I know, but I thought you would have heard," said Josie, "two senior officers received notice last Friday that the IOPC was investigating them. But, of course, nobody knows what it's about, but the rumour up here is that one of them died at the weekend."

"Dead? How?" asked Ricky. This conversation wasn't going the way he expected.

"She killed herself before whatever it was came out."

"You mean Plunkett, the Chief Constable in Ferris's area?"

"Exactly," said Josie, "she told Suzie to leave her phone, tablet and laptop at home when she attended the computer course. It made no sense to me. Sandra Plunkett must have been hiding something, and it sounds like that kidnapping was another attempt to keep a lid on it."

"Any idea where the other senior officer came from?" asked Ricky. "Same county or elsewhere in the country?"

"He's from Portishead," said Josie, "on gardening leave, waiting for the soft-shoe brigade to conclude their investigation. But, look, what's this about? I thought Mike Farrell was on that job, you know, hunting for the kidnapper?"

"Farrell? He's from Leek Wootton, isn't he? I haven't bumped into him yet. No big surprise, though; we're covering a huge area."

"What was the reason for the call, anyway?" asked Josie. "You must have wanted something more than a general chat."

"No, I got everything I needed, Josie," said Ricky and ended the call.

Chapter Three

DI MIKE FARRELL sat in an unmarked car near Fordyce Road. Beside him was Deepak Patel.

"This spot is close to the last known address for Gardiner's father, isn't it, guv?" asked Deepak.

"Yeah, George Gardiner lived two streets over, but that was years ago. So we've got people watching each of the addresses his former employers had on file for our man," said Mike. "The problem is Ricky spent so much time undercover with little or no contact with his handler; they aren't sure how many other places he might frequent."

"Needle and haystack," said Deepak.

"Tell me about it. There's enough CCTV coverage in the capital to find Lord Lucan, but Ricky Gardiner knows his way around. All we've had so far is three unconfirmed sightings. One of those was in Pinner two days ago. Our guys never found a trace of him there. The other two were so far out in the suburbs they felt wrong. So I guess he'll stick to the heart of this city he knew so well."

"Where to now, guv?" asked Deepak.

"Let's try a drive around," said Mike, "Crofton Park, Honor Oak and Forest Hill. We'll give it an hour and then return to base. We need the Met to dig deeper into Ricky's undercover identities. They must have names he used that link to a flat or property around here somewhere. He's not sleeping rough or in his car. There's been no sighting of that car since we got here. At least we traced the garage where he bought the cheap Audi. It travelled into London around the same time as we knocked on the door of 186 Woodman Lane. After that, it disappeared."

"He's ditched it, guv," said Deepak. "Should we get local cops going from yard to yard hunting for a crushed Audi?"

"I hope it doesn't come to that," said Mike. "Even if we confined the search to the streets where he used to operate, it would take us until Christmas."

Deepak started the car and plotted a route on his sat-nav to start them on a loop that brought them back to where they now sat. Mike's phone rang.

"Mike, it's DI Josie Bennett from Snow Hill. I had a call from a copper called Tony Fernandez earlier. He said he was working with you in the search for Gardiner. I only spoke with him because Des Copson reckoned he was a good sort. They worked together years ago on an under-cover drugs operation."

"Tony Fernandez? I've never heard of him. What rank is he?"

"He never said. He was more interested in the fallout from the Suzie Ferris kidnapping. I'm afraid I told him about Sandra Plunkett. He knew nothing about it. That seemed odd if he was on the search team you're running."

"He must have used the name Fernandez while working undercover in the Midlands," said Mike. "That explains why Des Copson thought it was a genuine call. I reckon you spoke to Ricky Gardiner, Josie."

"Sorry, Mike. I should learn to keep my big mouth shut."

"You could have done us a favour, Josie. I've got a name now to match with local properties. Gardiner must have a flat somewhere the Met doesn't know about; otherwise, we would have caught up with him by now. Thanks for the call."

"Do we keep going on this loop, guv?" asked Deepak.

"No, head back to base, and we'll gather the troops. Someone must know where Tony Fernandez lays his head at night."

Deepak returned to Lewisham Police Station. Mike radioed the other teams to meet them there. The room the Met Police had set aside struggled to accommodate the ten officers that joined Mike Farrell and Deepak Patel. Once everyone squeezed inside, Mike updated them with the news from Snow Hill.

"DI Josie Bennett received a call around noon today from Tony Fernandez. He reckoned he was part of the team hunting Ricky Gardiner. We know that's bullshit. Five of you are local lads teamed with people I brought with me. Deepak stayed with me because he was born in the borough. So, I believe it was Ricky Gardiner checking where we're at with the case."

"Was Tony Fernandez an alter ego?" asked a voice at the back of the room.

"Danny, is it?" asked Mike.

"Yes, guv," came the reply.

"We must remember that Gardiner worked undercover with the Met for twenty years. He's on civvy street now, but everything he learned during that time is coming into play.

So I reckon we should start looking for Tony Fernandez. Does he own a property within a ten-mile radius of this building? Does he rent a flat or an apartment? I'll grab as many local uniforms as the chiefs can free up to go door to door. I want them in bars, betting shops, and nightclubs, asking for anyone who's heard of a guy called Tony Fernandez. We've got his description and an excellent photograph. We need to get it circulated to as many people as possible. Someone must know him."

Mike went in search of reinforcements. They needed extra feet on the ground. He knew it wouldn't be possible to get anything other than Police Community Support Officers, but at least they knew the right people to ask. It was better than nothing.

RICKY GARDINER HAD MADE his way from Blythe Hill Tavern to the Railway Telegraph on Stansted Road. He took his time, making sure nobody followed him, keeping in the shadows, away from any street cameras. Before he opened the door to go inside, he scanned the bar. There was nobody suspicious. Ricky was hungry, and this place served decent grub throughout the day. The Railway Telegraph was an excellent place to spend the afternoon. He'd wander up to Lessing Street at around six this evening to catch the person renting his flat when she got home from work. If his memory wasn't failing him, Zena Gardjy worked for London Transport. Ricky planned to spend two nights in her spare bedroom unless trouble came calling.

OVER IN LEWISHAM, Mike Farrell had got four bodies happy to work on for two hours after their shift ended. Of course, it wasn't enough, but he told them where to go and what questions to ask. Mike hoped they could complete a simple task even though they were tired and ready for bed.

Mike got the other five teams looking for Tony Fernandez on the books of the local landlords. That was a thankless task. So many properties these days were multiple occupancies, and few landlords could tell you hand on heart the names of everyone behind every locked door. Mike appreciated that half a million illegals had to sleep somewhere. While Gardiner was at large, that wasn't his concern. His only focus was getting Gardiner into custody. The teams reconvened at four o'clock as arranged.

"What have you got?" asked Mike.

"We might have just found something, guv," said Jammy, a member of Mike Farrell's Armed Response Unit. "There's a flat in Croydon rented to a Tony Fernandez who fits Gardiner's description. The letting agent I spoke with reckoned he was a long-term client. Good as gold, never been behind with the rent. Fernandez had contacted them, maybe three times in fifteen years, for running repairs to the place. The agent wished the rest of his clientele were as pleasant."

"Have we got someone sitting on this place now?" asked Mike.

"Chris is in an unmarked car with Danny," said Jammy, "they're keeping watch on the place. If Gardiner shows, then they'll call for backup. They won't move until you give the nod."

"Good. We can't assume Gardiner is unarmed," said Mike. "I'll make the necessary arrangements. We'll get armed support to Chris as soon as possible. If Gardiner is inside the property when we arrive, we'll wait until he comes out again. I don't want to break down the door and find a potential hostage in the flat. He'll be easier to arrest when he's back on the street. Whatever happens, though, it's his last hideout."

"Is a hostage a possibility then, guv?"

"Think about it," said Mike, "we know Gardiner's got more than one hidey-hole. Is he made of money? Can he afford to keep several rented properties and never fall behind with the rent? Maybe he takes in lodgers. I don't know; perhaps he moves a family in and makes them pay over the odds while he doesn't need the place. It doesn't feel right that he has vacant properties, just lying around across London."

"The best situation would be for him to turn up tonight when we've got everything in position," said Jammy.

"My experience of Gardiner so far suggests he won't make things that easy. Let's hope it's the right address to start with," said Mike. "Did anyone else find a Tony Fernandez on a letting listing anywhere?"

There was a chorus of negative replies.

"To be fair, they haven't finished checking every letting agent yet, guv," said Deepak, "I propose we carry on the search. The ARU personnel can leave as soon as you get the Met's green light. Then, the rest of our teams can keep looking."

"I agree," said Mike Farrell. "Well done, Jammy. Make sure you get the bank details from this letting agent for Fernandez. That monthly Direct Debit is coming from somewhere and needs to get linked to Ricky Gardiner. Make more copies of that photograph available. The letting agents you've contacted could provide us with several aliases of Ricky Gardiner to add to the list of money trails we need to follow."

Mike Farrell felt pleased with the progress they'd made

today. The address Jammy uncovered in Croydon sounded promising. But, could they get access to equipment that told if it was empty or occupied by a family?

He started calling his Met colleagues to get clearance for an Armed Response Unit to work on London's streets. The more they knew of what lay behind the front door, the better. It was even better if Gardiner did as Jammy said, stayed in a pub until closing time, and then walked into their waiting arms.

WHILE MIKE FARRELL MADE PREPARATIONS, Ricky Gardiner was still in the Railway Telegraph. He'd enjoyed a proper London pub lunch and kept his alcohol intake to a minimum. Ricky spent the afternoon watching the world go by, both inside the bar and out on the streets. He saw nothing that caused him to worry.

"Finished with this glass, darling?" asked Millie, the young barmaid.

A lull in trade late afternoon, and Millie's boss told her to clear the decks before the next rush when the offices shut. So she collected the empty glasses and wiped clean the tabletops. According to her boss, the few remaining stragglers in the bar were people with nothing to live for.

"I'll have a coffee," said Ricky, "you can manage that, can you?"

"Alright, keep your hair on. I've only got one pair of hands."

Millie wiped the top of Ricky's table with a wet rag.

"Careful," shouted Ricky, "stop splashing me with dirty water."

"Sorry, I'm sure," said Millie, who flounced behind the bar to fetch him a coffee.

"Two pounds fifty," she said when she returned.

Millie leaned across the table with her hand out, waiting for the money. Ricky knew her game. Millie undid another button on her blouse when she went behind the bar. If he put the coins in her hand now, he couldn't avoid appearing to be looking at her breasts. She would call him a pervert or a dirty old man, any excuse to get back at him for shouting at her. Ricky slid the coins across the damp tabletop.

"No tip?" asked Millie.

"Yeah," said Ricky, "don't ask two-fifty for something you give away free."

Millie took the money to the till. Ricky risked a sip from the cup of coffee. Not bad. He wondered how long before the penny dropped. He didn't have long to wait,

"You bastard," shouted Millie.

Her boss came out of his office.

"What's up? Did someone run off without paying?"

Millie shook her head; Ricky finished his coffee and headed for the toilets. The landlord hadn't finished with his young barmaid.

"Do them buttons up, Millie. People come here for a quiet drink, not a strip show."

Five minutes later, Ricky Gardiner stood outside the Railway Telegraph. Five o'clock.

He had time for a stroll along memory lane for a spot of sightseeing before making it back to Lessing Street to meet with Zena Gardjy. It had been a while since Ricky had checked out his old stamping ground. No doubt it had altered beyond recognition and not for the better.

Ricky had already walked quite a few of the main thoroughfares in the borough, making sure he kept a low profile. Forest Hill was crisscrossed with various streets, smaller offshoots, and often parallel roads. The majority offered a new and often unusual sight somewhere along their length. The weather was perfect for an early evening stroll.

Ricky made for Beadnell Road, which gave access to the Garthorne Nature Reserve. He'd often thought it would be a decent spot to bury a body. Ricky spent a few minutes admiring the unspoilt nature of the Reserve and wondered how the endangered stag beetles were coping these days. Funny how random thoughts sprang into your head. He must be soft in his old age.

Ricky made his way back towards civilisation via Bovill Road and onto Brockley Rise. The traffic was manic this time of day. Ricky noted a different place to visit tonight as he wasn't returning to the Railway Telegraph. The change of venue had nothing to do with that little tart, Millie; it just wasn't wise to use the same pub more than once.

Ricky passed the General Napier after he crossed the road. A genuine neighbourhood watering hole he'd visited while undercover. He didn't know whose name it carried, but that pub would be where he spent his evening.

As he passed St Saviour's Church, he wondered how many churches there were here, now that so many had closed. A mosque had opened to make up the numbers every time he returned. He hadn't been inside a church since they buried his father, and that was the first time since his parents dragged him kicking and screaming to get christened when he was a toddler.

Ricky was closing in on the target for his ramble. He'd played here as a boy. Lowther Hill and Duncombe Hill ran parallel, on either side of a private park leading up to Brockley View. When he reached the top of the hill, he looked back towards the enclosed space, the most attractive spot in the borough. Brockley Hill Park was a sizeable green space and a prime site that a developer would love.

Even though the space was only open to residents bordering the land between those parallel roads, it still helped make urban life more bearable. Another childhood memory surfaced as Ricky looked back down Lowther Hill Road.

When he was eight years old, he played with the lads on the estates, and green space was a great attraction. Francis Rossi lived around here then. He would have been nineteen, and Status Quo had taken off. So Rossi bought a four-bedroomed house on Lowden Hill, less than a mile from his childhood home. The guitarist's Mum and Dad couldn't afford a place of their own before the group scored their first hit, so they lived with young Francis's grandmother.

Each of the semi-detached houses on the road had a garden plus access to the communal forest. Ricky used to watch Rossi's Great Dane bound past him in the woods, nearly knocking him off his feet. That dog loved running outside. Rossi, not so much. Ricky allowed himself a smile at the memory. But, blimey, that was fifty years ago—time to head back to Lessing Street and wait for Zena before he got maudlin.

As soon as she appeared at the end of the street, Ricky could tell his tenant wasn't happy to see him. He hadn't called in the unwritten favour during the seven years Zena had rented the two-bedroomed flat. She knew it was always possible, but it became less and less likely that James Harlow would get in touch as time went on. So today, when she spotted him standing on the pavement outside the flat, she swore under her breath.

"Only two nights, I promise," said Ricky, "I won't be any bother. You won't know I'm there."

Zena Gardjy opened the door, and they climbed the stairs to the first-floor flat.

"How was Charing Cross today," asked Ricky, not that he was interested in her job as a ticket officer.

"Nothing changes with the public, Mr Harlow," replied Zena, "always moaning about delays, overcrowding, clapped-out rolling stock, and how much it costs."

"How many fare dodgers did you catch?"

"Eleven," said Zena, smiling for the first time. "Eight of them hadn't tapped on, trying to save the fare on a single journey. Three habitual offenders argued their way to an eighty-pound fine. Days like today mean that I collect enough to pay my wages. Look, I wasn't expecting this. I don't have any food for you."

"You don't have to feed me, Zena. I need the use of your shower in the morning after you've left for work. Same again on Thursday morning, and that'll be me done. I'll slam the door of the flat behind me on the way out."

Ricky could tell Zena wasn't happy with the thought of him being there overnight.

He couldn't bother to explain why he wasn't interested. He wouldn't have jumped into bed beside young Millie, let alone an overweight Polish lady three years older than him.

"What are you doing later?" asked Zena as she put her shopping in the fridge.

"I'm off to the pub after I've scrounged a coffee from you," said Ricky, "I'll get back after you've turned in, so I'll take the spare key."

"It's behind you on the wall, beside the calendar," said Zena. "I'm taking a shower now. It's been a long day. I've got a lock on the door, so don't get any ideas."

"I'll make myself a coffee after I drop my gear in the spare room," said Ricky.

Zena watched him go, and then as soon as the bedroom door closed, she called her daughter.

"Agnieszka? I need to stay over tonight. Is that okay? Don't worry. I'll tell you when I get there."

In the spare room, Ricky was listening for the shower running. He had hidden something in the loft space the last time he was here. The net could be closing, and the weapon would come in handy.

After she'd ended her phone call, Zena went to the bathroom, locked the door, and ran the shower.

Ricky already stood on a chair, accessing the loft space. The pistol and ammunition were still safely wrapped in cloth inside a plastic bag. He looked at the gun, threw the Woolworth's bag back into the loft, and quietly closed the hatch. Ricky hadn't realised it had been so long since he'd slept here. He'd wondered for a second who Zena was on about until he remembered using the Harlow background story when he was undercover in a people-trafficking gang.

Zena was moving around in the flat once more. Ricky prayed she was dressed and not wandering around in a gown with a towel over her wet hair. When he rejoined her in the kitchen, Zena wore an Iron Maiden t-shirt and jeans. She'd made him a cup of coffee.

"Cheers, Zena," he said, "hot and strong, just how I take it."

Zena took no notice and sat on her black leather sofa watching TV. It was the only comfortable chair in the flat. Ah well, he was going out for a few pints anyway. Thirty minutes later, he picked up the spare front door key and headed for the General Napier.

Zena didn't look up when he left. Ricky thought it must have been a soap he had never watched. He couldn't see the attraction. When Ricky was outside on the pavement, Zena watched him cross the road and disappear along Gabriel Street. She could go to her daughter's now.

Agnieszka and her three children lived in a flat a ten-minute walk away. Thank goodness it was in the opposite direction.

Ricky Gardiner had forgotten Zena already. He was two minutes from the Napier and looking forward to his first pint. As he walked up Bovill Road, he tried to decide what takeaway he fancied on his way back to the flat. First things first, get inside the pub and order a cold beer.

He took his usual precautions, checking there were no dodgy cars parked in the street or people who looked conspicuous. Coppers on surveillance thought they were invisible, but Ricky prided himself on spotting everyone, bar the highly experienced ones. He paused on the step before pushing the door open—just his luck. Tuesday night was a quiz night. Ah, well, it could be worse. It could be bingo.

Ricky found a quiet corner and settled in for the long haul. The landlord seemed a decent sort, and the quiz included a round on the Blitz. Ricky was too young to remember it, but his parents lived through it as they had many old-timers who frequented the pubs in the borough. Ricky reckoned he would have scored well on those questions if he'd bothered to join in.

There's a common misconception that Londoners dashed to the underground stations or the air-raid shelters whenever the Luftwaffe visited the East End. Sixty per cent of them slept at home, sometimes for good. St Saviour's, the church he passed earlier, took a hit, and in 1941 there was a spate of fires in the centre of Forest Hill. You had a job to see the scars now, but most streets around the General Napier suffered damage to a degree.

Ricky nudged the guy on his left when a question arose about the potential target during the Baby Blitz attacks of March 1944. There were five hundred fires in southeast

London that night. Ricky whispered the answer. "They would have loved to have hit the Bell Green Gasworks."

"Are you sure, mate?"

"I'm sure," said Ricky, "he's on the ball is your landlord. It's a topical question because there's a move by the company that owns the site to demolish those iconic gasholders. They've survived two World Wars and should get preserved."

Ricky carried on drinking and chatting with the locals. He'd stopped checking for unfamiliar faces by ten o'clock. As soon as they learned the results, the quiz crowd left, and Ricky saw that less than a dozen people were keeping him company by a quarter past ten.

He decided it was time to get to the fried chicken place up the road. Zena would be in bed already as she needed to be out of the flat by seven to start work at eight at Charing Cross.

The landlord nodded as he returned his empty glass to the bar.

"Bingo tomorrow night if you're interested," he said, "poker night on Thursday."

"I'll give tomorrow a miss," said Ricky as he left the Napier.

He had to wait a few minutes to get served in the takeaway. Then, when he negotiated Bovill Road and turned into Gabriel Street, he regretted not visiting the Gents before leaving the pub.

Ricky hurried along Lessing Street and got the keys from his pocket. Zena hadn't left on the outside light. He searched for the lock. Success, the door flew open, and he almost fell inside. The stairway was pitch black. Ricky ran his hand over the wall to his left and then to his right, searching for the light switch. It was no good. He needed to pee and turned to go back outside. He wondered where he'd seen the closest dark alleyway. Needs must when the bladder drives.

A dark shadow filled the doorway. Ricky looked up and saw a raised hand.

It was the last thing he saw.

IN CROYDON, Chris and Danny remained in the unmarked car waiting for Fernandez to appear. One street over, Mike and Deepak sat in an ARV with a six-man crew.

"Eleven o'clock, guv," said Chris, "the pubs are chucking out now. If Gardiner's sleeping here tonight, it won't be long before he shows."

"Just remember the plan," replied Mike via his radio mike, "we apprehend Gardiner before he gets inside the property. The Met advised me thirty minutes ago that they believe a Bangladeshi family of five are inside the flat. Mum, Dad, their two kids, and the guy's seventy-five-year-old mother."

"OK, guv," said Chris, "no lights on in the property now. All tucked up in bed."

"That must be cosy," said Danny, "with only two bedrooms."

"Hold on," said Chris, "is that movement I can see on the street corner?"

"Stand by," said Mike.

"False alarm. It's an urban fox on his late-night prowl."

"Okay, quieten down," said Mike when he heard groans from the ARU crew. They were itching for action.

"It's midnight now, guv," said Deepak, "should we stand down? We can get a team to relieve Chris and Danny. They can sit on the flat until morning, and we can try tomorrow night."

"This place felt right, didn't it?" said Mike, "we'll give it an hour in case Gardiner's found a club to visit. That will give me time to find a relief team. There's more action six miles north of here. I just heard a report of a flat fire in Honor Oak keeping the London Fire Brigade busy."

"Odds on, it's an old bloke who dropped off to sleep with a fag in his hand," said Deepak.

"At this time of night, it's more likely to be a chip pan fire," said Chris. "Someone getting home from the pub and fancying a chip butty but nodding off on the sofa."

"Keep your fingers crossed that there was nobody home," said Mike.

"Do we have an address, guv?" asked Deepak.

"I think I heard Lessing Street mentioned," said Mike.

"Well, that's not one we identified as a Tony Fernandez flat," said Danny. "A pity, Gardiner could have done us a favour and burned himself to death."

"Hold on," said Chris, "there was a name I put a question mark by when I checked a listing earlier today. A James Harlow, I'd seen it on another letting firm's listing and wondered whether it could be one of Ricky's undercover personas. I meant to check with the Met. That Lessing Street address rings a bell."

"I wouldn't mind getting over there to check," said Mike Farrell.

"Why don't we drive over with Chris, guv?" asked Deepak. "The Armed Response Unit can keep the flat under surveillance, and if Gardiner shows, which looks unlikely, they can arrest him."

"We'll come to you, Chris," said Mike, "sit tight. Be with you in two minutes."

After they joined Chris and Danny, they set off on the A212 for Honor Oak.

"Only a short trip, guv," said Danny, "we'll pass Crystal Palace's football ground in a minute. Other than that, it's a decent bit of road. At this time of night, we should be there in twenty minutes."

Chris found Lessing Street with no bother. There were more lights than on a Christmas tree. Two fire crews were attending, and uniformed police and paramedics milled around on the pavements. The roof was well ablaze and threatening to spread to the adjoining terraced properties.

"Who's in charge here?" Mike Farrell wondered.

"See that bloke with the red and white chequered tabard?" said Danny. "He's a sub-officer from the Command Unit. Check if it's a fully involved fire, which it looks like it is. He'll know whether persons are reported too."

Mike Farrell headed towards the guy with Command Support on his tabard.

Deepak tried to find the most senior police officer on the street. Chris and Danny waited in the car and watched the flames turning to black and grey billowing smoke as the two high-powered hoses did their stuff from the aerial appliances.

Mike and Deepak returned to the parked car. Chris and Danny got out and stood beside them on the opposite side of the road from the fire.

"Was there a report of people inside the flat?" asked Chris.

"The first floor is where the fire started," said Deepak. "It's occupied by a single female, Zena Gardjy, who hoped to celebrate her sixtieth birthday in October."

"Craig, the sub-officer called it a Class B fire," said Mike

Farrell, "which suggests flammable liquids. It's far too early to speculate, but when I suggested the word accelerant, he didn't tell me not to be stupid. He used the term fully involved, Danny. You were right."

"There's a uniformed Sergeant around somewhere," Deepak added, "making sure the public keep out of harm's way. The paramedics can't do a thing until they've got this fire under control. Although, unless a fireman injures himself, they're wasting their time."

"We're playing the waiting game again, just as in Croydon," said Mike. "How can we confirm that Harlow owned this flat and link it to Gardiner?"

"Mrs Gardjy has a daughter, according to one of her neighbours, guv," said Deepak. "the neighbour's stood over there in the black nightdress, with a fireman's jacket around her shoulders."

"I'll go," said Danny, "we need a name, address and telephone number if possible, am I right, guv?"

"For Mrs Gardjy's daughter, yes, Danny,"

"Of course, guv, that's what I meant, but you can't blame a bloke for trying."

Danny ran back two minutes later.

"Agnieszka is the daughter, guv. She lives up the road. I've asked the uniformed Sergeant to send someone around. Keely reckons the daughter has young kids."

"Keely? That's the girl with the nightdress, is it?" asked Deepak.

"Yeah, she's gone with the coppers. Keely offered to sit with the kids."

"Good neighbours," said Mike, "you can't beat them."

"True," said Danny, "but Keely was getting chilly over there, even with that jacket around her shoulders. Like organ stops, they were. I didn't know where to look."

Mike Farrell walked across to the Command Support officer for an update.

Activity on the aerial appliances was reducing. There was zero chance of entering the property tonight, but the danger of the fire spreading appeared over.

"Who's this arriving now, guv?" asked Chris.

Two women got out of a police car and stopped and stared at what remained of the first-floor flat across the road.

Mike Farrell led his team across to talk to them.

"Excuse me," he said, "I'm Detective Inspector Farrell. Are you Mrs Gardjy?"

The older lady in the Iron Maiden t-shirt and jeans nodded.

"What's happened here?" she said, clutching her daughter's arm.

"Neighbours thought you were inside. But, thank God, it appears the flat was empty."

"Where's Mr Harlow?" asked Zena Gardjy. "He was sleeping here tonight. I've not seen hide nor hair of him in the seven years I've rented the place, and he turned up tonight and said he was staying for two nights."

"Mr James Harlow?" asked Mike. Zena Gardjy nodded.

"Is this the gentleman, Mrs Gardjy?" asked Deepak Patel, showing her a photograph.

"That's him," she said, "he was going to the pub and had the spare key."

Zena had just identified Ricky Gardiner as her landlord.

The Command Support officer trotted up to join them.

"The firefighter on the left-hand aerial appliance reported a body in the kitchen, Mike."

"Thanks, Craig."

Curiouser and curiouser, thought Mike.

It would be morning before he could confirm the identity of the person inside, but it appeared they'd caught up with Ricky Gardiner at last.

Someone wanted him dead and had spread highly flammable material around the kitchen to destroy as much evidence as possible.

Chapter Four

Wednesday, 6 June 2018

GUS HOPED today was a better day than yesterday. As he left the driveway of his bungalow, the signs looked promising. The cloud and drizzle that dogged the county over the past twenty-four hours had gone. Instead, bright sunshine prevailed, and temperatures climbed into the low twenties Celsius.

Rapid mental arithmetic confirmed that even Fahrenheit meant it was warm enough to leave his jacket in the wardrobe. At least there was still space on the rail for his coats. How long that continued was still unknown. Suzie started back to work half day from today.

Another unknown was who killed Mark Malone. The team worked long hours yesterday identifying witnesses to contact for an interview. Gus knew he hadn't entirely concentrated on the cold case while other matters were unresolved.

When he left the Old Police Station office at five o'clock yesterday, there had been no whisper about progress by Mike Farrell and his crew in the hunt for Ricky Gardiner. They had scoured London since the middle of last week, and apart from the odd spurious sighting, they'd missed him.

The lack of news on Gardiner didn't help Gus's mood. The events of last weekend already troubled him. Culverhouse and Plunkett received official notification on Friday morning of their suspension pending an IOPC investigation into serious misconduct. The officers involved reacted in different ways.

Chief Constable Sandra Plunkett tidied her office and drove home to a cottage in the country a few miles from Lichfield. There, she joined her partner, Naomi Hall. Gus could only speculate over the conversations that followed. He learned the outcome on Monday morning when the ACC called him to the London Road HQ.

Sandra Plunkett had helped conceal a hit-and-run death that occurred in September 2012. Naomi Hall was an innocent party. She wasn't with Sandra at that senior officers' reunion weekend. However, the prospect of Sandra's career coming to an inglorious end proved too much for both partners to take. The two women committed suicide, and the emergency services personnel discovered them side by side, holding hands, in their garage.

Assistant Chief Constable, Dominic Culverhouse, worked until the end of the day. Then, he left the Avon and Somerset HQ in Portishead to spend the weekend at home near Hereford. Culverhouse exercised his right to transfer to another force until the IOPC investigation concluded. Whereas Sandra Plunkett spoke with nobody at Devizes before she left, Culverhouse was at great pains to tell his colleagues that he had nothing to hide. Culverhouse stressed this allegation was a figment of someone's bitter imagination.

The Acting Chief Constable called Gus at home yesterday evening to inform him that Culverhouse would attend a meeting on Friday. The preliminary meeting at Portishead would hear evidence and decide whether it required a misconduct hearing.

Gus drove into the car park below the CRT office and parked. As he got out of his old Focus, he spotted Luke Sherman arriving.

"Good morning, Luke," he said.

"It is, guv," said Luke, "and long may it continue."

They rode in the lift together and found Lydia Logan Barre had beaten them to it.

"You just missed DS Mercer, guv," she said.

"Here or on the phone?" asked Gus.

"On the phone, guv. You need to turn straight around and drive back to Devizes. There were developments overnight."

Gus sighed and headed for the lift.

"We'll start arranging those interviews, guv," said Luke.

"I'll chase the Hub for the outstanding research they're handling for us," added Lydia.

Gus waved a hand in acknowledgement.

He'd known it was too good to last. The trip into town had gone too smoothly, and now every known hot spot teemed with traffic for the return journey. It took fifty minutes before he escaped the oppressive heat of the interior of his Focus and climbed the steps to the door of the HQ building.

A glance showed the ACC expected him at least fifteen minutes earlier. But, instead, he glowered at him from his first-floor office window. Gus imagined it was a glower. Difficult to tell with the glare of the sun in his eyes.

Geoff Mercer wasn't at the top of the stairs waiting for him this morning. Instead, he stood right inside the main door and immediately grabbed his arm.

"Don't bother signing in," he said, dragging Gus towards the stairs, "I've filled in your details. You can initial them on your way out. The ACC didn't want you getting waylaid by the admin staff."

The opportunity to chat with Vera Butler and Kassie Trotter highlighted many of Gus's visits to London Road. The ACC must have something important to impart. Gus hoped it was news that Ricky Gardiner was under lock and key.

Geoff and Gus made it through the ACC's office door with no one stopping them. Kenneth Truelove turned away from the window and sat in his chair.

"A Metropolitan Police surgeon is examining a body recovered from a flat fire in Honor Oak Park this morning," he said. "DI Mike Farrell suspects it's Ricky Gardiner."

"How will they tell?" asked Gus.

"Dental records," said Geoff Mercer, "the body got badly burned."

"London Fire Brigade will confirm later today whether it was arson," said the ACC. "DI Farrell said a sub-officer at the scene told him there was large-blister charring which showed that the fire developed rapidly and generated high temperatures. There were signs of a liquid accelerant. The irregular burn patterns suggested that someone had poured a flammable liquid on the kitchen floor and worktops."

"Perhaps Gardiner killed the flat owner and disappeared?" asked Gus.

"The lady renting the flat spent the night with her daughter. Since they've been in London, Farrell and his team learned that Gardiner had several properties to allow him to lie low. It appears he sublet most of those for a reasonable sum with one proviso. So if Gardiner ever needed a bed for the night, they had to accommodate him. Mrs Gardjy, the lady who rented the two-bedroomed flat in Honor Oak, told Mike her guest was staying a maximum of two nights. She knew him as James Harlow but was uncomfortable sleeping under the same roof, so she went to her daughter's as soon as Ricky left for the pub. Mike Farrell also unearthed the name, Tony Fernandez, as another identity Gardiner assumed from time to time."

"If it was Gardiner in that fire, someone killed him and tried to destroy any evidence that might lead back to them," said Geoff Mercer.

"Who do we know that wanted Gardiner dead?" asked Gus.

"You're not seriously suggesting Culverhouse had anything to do with it, are you?"

"Why not, Geoff?" said Gus, "Sandra Plunkett's dead."

"It makes perfect sense," agreed the ACC. "We sent evidence to the IOPC showing that he and Plunkett were in a car which hit Jason Whitworth and failed to stop. Gardiner murdered Terry Davis to prevent that secret from getting uncovered. We are relying on the IOPC to find the money trail which proved Culverhouse and Plunkett paid Gardiner to get rid of Davis."

"That was the only potential flaw in the package we sent to the IOPC," said Geoff. "As far as our two colleagues were concerned, the truth about what occurred on that road back in 2012 was enough to ruin their careers. That degree of serious misconduct would get them dismissed from service. Criminal charges relating to the hit-and-run would follow. The icing on the cake was proving beyond doubt that they hired Gardiner to kill Terry Davis."

"Culverhouse and Plunkett might have covered the money trail so well that the IOPC could never link them to the murder," said the ACC.

"We caught Gardiner in half a dozen spots in Devizes on the night in question," said Gus. "He was a mercenary, based on testimony from his former colleagues at the Met. We know he left for London from Chippenham station after walking from Devizes, and the timing fits for the murder. What we can't do is put Gardiner at the top of that fire escape pushing Terry to his death."

"What you're saying is," said the ACC, "a good brief might well get him off the murder charge."

"We had one other thing to add," said Gus, "Terry's phone. Neil collected it from Chippenham station. Gardiner handed it in with a story he'd found it in the car park. Forensics didn't find any fingerprints to prove Gardiner handled it, as we suspected would be the case, and there was nothing concerning the case on the phone. But, again, there was no doubt it was Gardiner. A station staff member identified him from a photograph, but anyone could have found the phone in Devizes and dropped it at the station. It might look suspicious, but a good brief could say it was only circumstantial."

"There was so much that only added up once you accepted our explanation of how things went. Despite that, everything hinged on the money trail to close the loop," agreed Geoff. "We can't do every job. We handed what we'd gathered on the murder to Warwickshire Police to treat it as a prelude to Suzie Ferris's kidnapping. If they'd caught and arrested him, Gardiner was going to prison for that anyway."

"Let's analyse this for a minute and forget the triumvirate for now," said Gus. "We gave the IOPC enough evidence to nail Culverhouse and Plunkett on the hit-and-run. Agreed?"

Geoff Mercer and Kenneth Truelove nodded their agreement.

"DCI Oliver Pinnock at Leek Wootton had the evidence to charge Gardiner with kidnapping Suzie once they made an arrest. Do you see any flaws there?"

"None," said Geoff. The ACC shook his head.

"Except that they can't charge a dead man," he said. "If the body in the flat was Ricky Gardiner."

"True, but someone at the IOPC and Leek Wootton should ask the obvious questions," said Gus. "Why was Terry Davis murdered? Why did Gardiner kidnap Suzie? Even the dimmest detective would realise there was more to it."

"Without proof that Gardiner committed both crimes and a money trail leading to Culverhouse and Plunkett, it will be impossible to implicate them in any other crime than the hit-and-run," said the ACC.

"Could you console yourself with the prospect of Culverhouse serving a minimum of eight years in prison, Gus?" asked Geoff.

"I suppose so, Geoff," Gus replied. "Where is Culverhouse?"

"He applied to transfer out of Avon and Somerset for the duration of the investigation," said the ACC. "I'll make enquiries."

"Do you want me for anything else?" asked Gus, "I need to rally the troops on this Mark Malone case."

The ACC was already on the phone. Geoff followed Gus to the door.

"What a strange week," said Geoff, "I never liked our Chief Constable, but I wouldn't have wished her dead. Ricky Gardiner was a nasty piece of work, and there won't be many tears shed if it turns out he was in that fire. Yet I can't help wishing he was still alive. Gardiner's death could destroy several loose ends we needed to tie up to clinch the case against Culverhouse. But, of course, nothing is ever straightforward, is it?"

"Morning, Mr Freeman," called Kassie, "are you dashing off without a word?"

"Mr Freeman's busy, Kassie," said Geoff Mercer, "as you ought to be. The ACC hasn't had his mid-morning coffee yet. Nor have I come to think of it."

"Vera's delivered your refreshments to your office, Mr Mercer," said Kassie. "Suzie Ferris is waiting for you. She's supposed to be doing afternoons only this week, but she wondered if there was any news on that Gardiner bloke. I'll sort out the ACC now you're both out of the way. He might enjoy getting his teeth into one of my bonbons."

Geoff and Gus shared a glance. That sounded far worse than it was in reality.

"I'd better update Suzie," said Geoff as Kassie went to see Kenneth Truelove. "You get back to your CRT people, Gus. No doubt, there will be further updates from Mike Farrell before the day's out."

Geoff disappeared into the gloomy passageway leading to his office. Gus wanted to follow him to see Suzie. Vera was bringing empty cups from the opposite side of the admin area and stopped for a chat.

"What is it this time?" she asked, "whenever you turn up at London Road, there's always unpleasant news."

"An unconfirmed report that Ricky Gardiner died in a fire in London overnight. It looks like murder."

"What a mess," said Vera, "that only leaves Dominic Culverhouse."

"Convenient, don't you think?" said Gus. "Sorry, I can't stop, Vera. I need to get back to work."

"Another time?" she asked.

"Definitely," said Gus, "this business will be over one day."

Vera watched Gus descend the stairs and sign out. Then she walked back to the kitchen. Kassie joined her thirty seconds later with more dirty cups and saucers.

"You wash, and I'll wipe," said Kassie. "How was Mr Freeman? Did you snatch a word with him?"

"Half a dozen, at most."

"Are you okay?" asked Kassie.

"Oh, I'll get over it," said Vera, "I'm taking my first steps tomorrow night when a few of us are meeting for a drink in the Bear."

"Back in the ranks of the FEW, Vera, who'd have thought, eh?" said Kassie. "If I don't find someone soon, I'll forge the necessary documents and join you."

"Perhaps we could arrange an honorary membership," said Vera. "because you don't qualify as an ex-wife."

WHEN GUS REACHED the Old Police Station office, he updated Lydia and Luke with the news from London. But, unfortunately, there was nothing they could do to influence matters. Mike Farrell was running the operation, which would end once he knew the autopsy result.

Gus wondered how Suzie took the news that there could be nobody to charge for her kidnapping. It was an unsatisfactory ending and no mistake. Gus imagined that John and Jackie Ferris would feel the same way.

"How many identities did Gardiner have, guv?" asked Lydia.

"I'm not sure anyone knows," said Gus, "once Mike Farrell and his crew return to Warwickshire, I guess they'll lose interest in chasing any more information. I'd hope the Met would try to unravel the mystery. If Kenneth Truelove were on the ball, he'd be badgering them to continue chasing the money."

"Alex's background check on Gardiner's family threw up several properties his late mother owned, didn't it?" asked Luke.

"Gardiner was selling everything off, Luke," said Gus, "I expect he planned to make a new life abroad, as many do, living in the lap of luxury. That didn't work out well for him if he died in that fire last night."

"Are you ready to hear the list of interviewees, guv?" asked Luke.

"Are we talking to the Bath-based people first?"

"Yes, guv, we can tackle the Newbury list tomorrow or Friday."

"We could drop by the JET garage on the way back to work out what might have gone on there. Was that the spark that lit the flame, or was it a slow burn from Newbury?"

"We will need to spread the net wider, guv," said Lydia, "I've traced the names of gang members who could have attacked Mark Allison. One of those men could have inherited the weapon used to kill Mark Malone."

"Or it could have made its way to someone with no

connection to any of the above," said Gus, "but it's a start. So, OK, read them and weep."

"Jenny Malone was Mark's mother. She's fifty-four years of age and divorced. She runs an employment agency in Bath. The family home is in Combe Down."

"Mark wasn't living at home, was he?" asked Gus.

"No, guv," said Luke, "he lived alone in a swish flat off Marlborough Lane, near the Royal Crescent."

"Swish, Luke?" asked Gus, "have you been there?"

Luke looked flustered for a second but composed himself.

"I didn't know Mark, guv. I was already with Nicky in 2015. However, I've visited the area often. We have friends who live in the Royal Crescent. It has high exclusivity, and properties in nearby Marlborough Lane, both old and new, have gained a certain cachet through their proximity."

"Very nice, I'm sure," said Gus, "does Combe Down possess the same cachet?"

"Not quite, guv," said Luke, "but Jenny Malone owns a detached three-bedroomed house with a double garage that would fetch three-quarters of a million if it came on the market."

"We should talk to Jenny Malone first," said Gus, "we need far more background on our victim than we've got in the murder file."

"I've just got the detailed phone records back from the Hub we wanted, guv," said Lydia. "I can show you Mark Malone's complete contact list and who he got in touch with in the forty-eight hours before he died."

"I'll study the detail later, Lydia, when it's available in the Freeman Files. Can you give me the highlights? I want to get a feel for the guy."

"Malone had around two hundred contacts on his

phone. A rough estimate would be that forty percent of those are related to his pet shop business. His family and friends comprised around the same number. Mark was a gregarious young man with a wide circle of friends and a great love of dogs. I don't recall it in the murder file, but Mark Malone bred specialist breeds and showed them at Crufts. He was successful without ever taking home the ultimate prize. Up to forty names on his phone were people and organisations from the Kennel Club world."

"That's interesting," said Gus, "but it doesn't explain how he could afford such an expensive car. Nor why Mark got shot with a murder weapon once owned by a London gang member. I'm not au fait with the doggie world, but it doesn't strike me as the community where I'd expect to rub shoulders with someone from organised crime."

"Can't agree there, guv," said Luke. "These show dogs can be expensive enough to attract criminals. I read a report last month of three puppies stolen from a house in Leicester. One was a Best in Breed at last year's Crufts and valued over twenty thousand pounds. The other two were worth around three thousand pounds each."

"What would the thieves do with them?" asked Gus. "Is there a market? Because surely, animals such as these get microchipped, don't they? So there would be no chance of the thieves showing the dogs in competitions themselves."

"Perhaps they believed that champions bred champions, guv," said Lydia, "like racehorses. So if they couldn't sell them on, it might mean they would destroy them. How horrible."

"Even if the police found the three dogs, the owners thought their competition days were at an end," said Luke. "These animals are temperamental, and a traumatic disruption to their routine could prove devastating."

"Not as devastating as for the owners," said Lydia, "I bet they are desperate to get them home. Owners of common dog breeds can treat their pets as family members. Heaven knows how important those dogs were to that Leicester family."

"Was there any further information in the article you read, Luke, concerning the puppy trade?" asked Gus. He was ready to admit a total lack of knowledge of what went on in this business.

"The European Union was getting involved in the booming puppy trade scandal even before Mark Malone's death, guv. This trade isn't exclusive to Britain; illegal trade is rife across Europe. They require eight million puppies each year to supply the demand. That makes online trade worth over one billion euros."

"I can see where organised crime fits into this scenario now," said Gus, "I didn't realise it was such a lucrative pastime."

"The trade has an enormous impact on the health and welfare of the dogs involved," said Luke. "The internal market gets hit too through unfair competition, tax evasion, consumer rights and public health. An international animal charity called for a conference to tackle the illegal trade where vets, breeders, lawyers, politicians, and representatives from non-profit organisations examined the challenges and thrashed out solutions. The ultimate aim was to convince the Union for appropriate regulation."

"Just what we need," said Lydia, "more red tape from the EU."

"The number of dogs smuggled across Europe has rocketed since the turn of the century," said Luke. "People are demanding certain breeds, more exotic breeds than we used to own. The pet passport system currently in operation doesn't work. Nowadays, it's so easy to buy or sell a puppy online, and the seller is the only winner. The animals get transported thousands of miles in unsatisfactory conditions. They're at high risk of transmissible disease; if they survive, they can become too difficult for the new owner to manage. As a result, they get abandoned."

"It sounds like your typical online scam adept at making money out of gullible pet lovers," said Gus.

"By 2016, it was the third most profitable organised crime within the EU after drugs and guns, guv," said Luke.

"Could this be how that weapon linked to Mark Malone?" asked Lydia, "was he involved in buying litters of certain breeds getting smuggled into the country? Those breeds in the highest demand? Do you remember Obama's Portuguese Water Dogs?"

"I can't say they ever registered, Lydia," said Gus. "They sound like an indie shoegazing band from the 1990s, but carry on; I might hear a name I recognise in time."

"People want to own dogs that they see celebrities pictured with guv," said Luke, "the Doberman Pinscher has been a favourite for a while. However, if you enjoy carrying your little darling around town, then the Alaskan Klee Kai or a White Maltese might suit you."

"I think not," said Gus, "I reckon you two might be a better fit for several of these upcoming interviews."

"It will be a walk in the park, guv," said Lydia. Luke groaned.

Gus's phone rang. "Saved by the bell," he said. It was the ACC.

"Still no confirmation on the identity of our flat fire victim, Freeman. However, I've discovered where Culverhouse transferred to last week. He went to Greenwich."

"The next borough to Lewisham, and the right side of

the river for easy access to Croydon. Culverhouse knew Gardiner better than we did. How far was he from the flat?"

"Five miles," said the ACC, "it's hard to believe he's capable of murder, but there's no denying motive and potential opportunity. I could contact Greenwich to check where Culverhouse was on the night in question, to rule him in or out?"

"Even as a suspended ACC, you can bet he wasn't walking the beat," said Gus, "my guess is he finished at five o'clock and stalked Gardiner until closing time. Then he struck when Ricky was most vulnerable. I'd expect the Met surgeon to find blunt-force trauma to the back of Ricky's skull. Forensics will have found blood at the foot of the stairs to match with Gardiner's records and show that the body got dragged upstairs and was doused in petrol and set alight."

"That sounds plausible, but just as with Terry Davis's murder, we need solid evidence."

"Yes, Sir," said Gus, "and we're not dealing with an amateur who will make silly mistakes. If it was Culverhouse, as I suspect, then he outwitted Ricky Gardiner. No mean feat, considering the man's years of experience on the force. We've mentioned this already; Gardiner wrote the manual for several of the 'how to' operations detectives carry out day-to-day."

"I've passed this information on to DCI Pinnock at Leek Wootton," said the ACC. "We must leave things in their capable hands as they liaise with the Met on the flat fire investigation."

"I'll wait to hear from you on the body ID," said Gus, "I'm off to Bath after lunch for a chat with our victim's mother."

"The Malone case? How does it look? Done and dusted by Friday?"

"I would have to be barking mad to promise you that, Sir," said Gus. "We haven't got a sniff of a motive yet, let alone a list of suspects."

"You've said that before, Freeman, then like a magician pulling a rabbit out of the hat, you produce the answer."

"I admire your confidence, Sir, and I look forward to hearing from you later."

With that, the ACC rang off, and Gus wondered how on earth they would get an answer for *next* Friday, let alone in the next two days.

"Back to the grindstone, guv?" asked Lydia.

"Where were we? Ah, yes, the highlights from Malone's contact list. Give me the last six calls or texts on the night he died."

"At six-fifteen pm, Mark texted Damian New, the friend from Newbury he was visiting. Mark rarely identified people in his contact list with their surnames. Instead, it was a first name, location, or a reminder of what they did for a living. Damian New's full name is Damian Hartley-Cole, thirty-seven, an interior designer. The guy who cleans his shop windows was Paul Chammy."

"Moving swiftly on," said Gus.

"Sorry, guv," said Lydia, "the message read 'Leaving now. Can't wait to see you xxx.' Damian received and read the message. At six-fifty pm, Mark received a call from his mother. He had hands-free in his BMW; they spoke for one minute forty seconds."

"We'll ask what they discussed when we see her," said Gus, "carry on."

"At eight o'clock, Mark received a text from Julian Shih Tzu asking whether Mark was showing this year at Paws In

The Park. Mark called Julian back at five past. That conversation lasted fifteen seconds."

"Details on Julian? Did someone ask whether the answer was yes, or no? Would it matter, I wonder?"

"Julian Drummond, forty-three years old, is a photographer who lives in Milton Keynes."

"I'm surprised he didn't show bulldogs," said Gus.

Gus saw Lydia's puzzled look. The ignorance of youth.

"There was a long gap then while Mark was in Newbury at Damian's party."

"Ah, we know that was why he travelled to Newbury, do we? Who told us that? It wasn't in the murder file. It merely stated that Mark had visited friends in Newbury, and I assumed there were at least two people at the property."

"Mark's mother mentioned a party when I called to arrange the interview, guv," said Luke.

"OK, that's something else to follow up on when we see her," said Gus.

"The next call came at fifteen minutes to midnight, guv," said Lydia, "hands-free again. Mark spoke to Patrick Circus for two minutes."

"All right, you needn't explain," said Gus, "it's not what he does for a living. Patrick has a flat on The Circus, in Bath."

"Yes, guv," said Lydia, "Patrick Boddington, fifty-five years old, a fine arts dealer with a gallery next to the Abbey. Mark and Patrick often visited fashionable bars and restaurants together; however, the exact nature of their relationship was unclear. Mark called Patrick back five minutes after midnight."

"When Mark had stopped at the JET garage?" asked Gus.

"The timing fits, guv," said Luke.

"How long did that call last?"

"Seven minutes, guv," said Lydia.

"Put Patrick Boddington on the list for first thing tomorrow. I need to know what they spoke about."

"That's it, guv," said Lydia. "No more texts or phone calls."

"Well, that's a couple of leads to follow," said Gus, "but still no sign of a link to something criminal. We'll delve further back into Mark's call history another time. Luke, can you ring Jenny Malone, please? Tell her to expect us in forty-five minutes. Lydia, you're with me for this visit. Are you ready to leave now?"

"I'll nip to the loo, guv. See you downstairs."

Lydia disappeared to the restroom.

"How do you see this case, Luke?" asked Gus. "Can you offer any insight?"

"If you mean because I'm gay, then, no, I can't, guv. Is that why I'm not coming with you this time? Do you think Mark's mother will recognise me, or I'll remind her of her son?"

"We are what we are, Luke," said Gus as Lydia re-emerged in the office. "If you can offer something that will help progress this case, then don't hold back. We're a team with different skills and life experiences. I never want you to feel you need to qualify any contribution you make in our conversations or the reports you include in the Freeman Files. Something you leave out altogether or imply is less important could be vital. I'm only interested in results, Luke. This team has to solve cases to continue to exist. I'll have your back one hundred per cent if someone is out of line. That goes for Alex, Neil, Lydia, and anyone else who might work here."

"Understood, guv," said Luke.

Gus headed for the lift. Lydia followed him.

"Did I miss something, guv?" she asked as they reached the ground floor.

"Time will tell, Lydia," said Gus, "let's talk to Jenny Malone.

In the CRT office, Luke Sherman was making a phone call.

"Nicky? Sorry to call you at work. Patrick Boddington? What can you tell me?"

Chapter Five

THE DRIVE TO Combe Down took thirty minutes. Gus pulled up outside an elegant-looking detached property built in the 1930s.

"I wonder when they added the double garage extension?" asked Lydia. "Ten years ago, do you think?"

"The planners in historical cities such as Bath demand that any building alteration is in keeping with their surroundings. Sympathetic is a word that often crops up. In the Royal Crescent, owners have a minimal palette to choose from for the colour of their front door. You won't find a triple-glazed window within a mile. It's the original Georgian sash window or nothing."

"It appears the planners are less strict up here on the hill."

"Bath is all hills, Lydia," said Gus, "the Romans built Aqua Sulis here because seven hills surround the city in the valley. It reminded them of home."

"It looks like a beautiful place to live, guv," said Lydia, "even if Jenny Malone lives alone."

Gus rang the doorbell. The chimes echoed along the hallway. Finally, he saw the owner walking from the kitchen through the glass-panelled front door.

"You must be the police? Come into the lounge."

Gus and Lydia stepped into the hallway and followed Jenny Malone through the door to the right. Lydia closed the front door behind them.

Mark's mother was as elegant as the fixtures and fittings which adorned her living room. Jenny Malone was tall, immaculately dressed, and her hair cut stylishly short. Lydia didn't doubt for a second that the string of pearls around her neck would cost her a month's wages.

Jenny Malone sat in a chair by the mock Regency fireplace and waited for Gus to speak.

"Mrs Malone," said Gus, "thank you for agreeing to speak with us. My name is Freeman, and I am a consultant with Wiltshire Police. My Crime Review Team is taking a second look at the murder of your son, Mark, back in May 2015. Unfortunately, it wasn't possible to determine who killed Mark at the time, nor was an acceptable motive established. We hope to do better this time. My colleague here is Ms Logan Barre."

"What a lovely name," said Jenny Malone, "where do you come from, my dear?"

"Aberdeen," replied Lydia.

"I see," said Jenny Malone.

"It must be painful for you to go through this again, Mrs Malone," said Gus, "three years is no time after losing someone close to you."

"My only son and I weren't as close as I would have liked, Mr Freeman. Mark moved into a place of his own when he was twenty. His father had left within a month of Mark coming out on his eighteenth birthday. Gerry was a bigot, and I knew that fact when I married him. But it didn't seem important. Gerry and I met at the Rec during the rugby season and married the following Spring. I was twenty, Gerry was thirty-two. Mark arrived ten months later, a honeymoon baby, and Gerry couldn't have been happier. He was desperate for a son who would follow Bath Rugby as he did. Perhaps play for the club in years to come. Before Mark became a teenager, Gerry realised his son was different. He tried hard to change and mould him into the budding sportsperson he craved. Mark disappointed him, so Gerry ignored him and me. My ex-husband threw himself into his work as an architect with a local firm. His working days grew longer and longer, and the inevitable happened. One month after Mark sat us down to tell us he was gay, Gerry calmly announced he was leaving me for another woman. Her name was irrelevant. She was the latest in a long line of girls with whom he'd cheated. Gerry took no responsibility for his behaviour, nor did he say I drove him to it. Everything was Mark's fault. Gerry couldn't accept that he'd fathered someone so effeminate. Gerry sat in that chair where you are, Mr Freeman, and asked how I thought it made him look. As if people thought less of him because his son was gay. I was happy to see the back of him. Gerry didn't even come to Mark's funeral."

"I appreciate you filling in the background for us," said Gus. "When we pick up an unsolved case from several years earlier, we don't always have the full story in our records. Later, there may be questions relating to the period between his eighteenth birthday and the weeks before his death. Can we concentrate for now on the night in question? For instance, Mark's phone records show that you rang him while he travelled between Bath and Newbury. A call that you made at around ten minutes to seven. Do you remember what you spoke about?"

"It was the last time I spoke to Mark, Mr Freeman," said Jenny Malone, "I'm hardly likely to forget. I asked if he was coming to dinner on Sunday. I didn't ask him every week because Mark had turned me down too often. But, on this occasion, he said yes, unless he got a better offer. I was grateful that he didn't dismiss the invitation out of hand and looked forward to it. I told Mark I loved him and hoped he had a great time at the party."

"This would be a party in Newbury, at the home of Damian Hartley-Cole, is that correct?" asked Gus.

"That's right," said Jenny, "how much do you know about parties, Mr Freeman?"

"It's been a long time since I went to one," said Gus.

"I doubt you've ever been to one like that," said Jenny.

"Mark liked to play, Mrs Malone. Is that what you're saying?" asked Lydia.

Jenny Malone nodded.

"I worried about him keeping healthy, but Mark always told me not to fuss. He said he could look after himself. I begged him to settle down and find himself a partner. When he first came out, he spent time with Patrick, but it was never loving, just lust."

"Patrick? That would be Patrick Boddington, I take it?" asked Gus.

"Yes, Patrick likes younger men. He had lots of money, and an impressionable beginner could soon fall under his spell. He makes them feel special. Mark looked at Patrick as a teacher, and although they still met up for a meal, there was no sex anymore. Mark was too old."

"When did Mark leave school?" asked Gus, "I mean full-time education. Did he leave at sixteen or eighteen?"

"Oh, Mark was an intelligent lad. He passed three A-Levels with good grades. Enough to get him into university, but he was already working in the pet shop at weekends and holidays. Mark adored all domestic animals, not just dogs. When he left King Edward's school, he announced he was starting full-time as an Assistant Manager. Nothing I said persuaded him otherwise. Mark took over the running of the shop around six years later."

"When did Mark start showing dogs in competitions?" asked Lydia. "Which specialist breeds was he showing?"

"The previous manager of the pet shop was the experienced breeder. She encouraged Mark to follow in her footsteps. You would need to talk to someone else about that side of his life. I'm not a dog lover. Is it important? I can't imagine his killer being someone jealous of Mark's dog being reserve champion in one of the obscure classifications at Crufts."

"Could we speak to the previous manager of the pet shop?" asked Gus.

"Through a medium," said Jenny Malone. "There's an alternative therapy business on the premises now. Tamsin Sheridan owned and managed the shop for years. Tamsin retired when she was confident Mark could run the place single-handed. When Mark died, she wasn't well enough to pick up the reins again. The shop stayed closed for a while, then Tamsin died, and that was that."

"Maybe we should talk to another dog show participant," said Gus, "have you ever met Julian Drummond?"

"Mark mentioned him. They were great rivals and avoided one another like the plague. Anyone who is anyone attends Crufts, but several smaller shows take place around the country. If Mark entered a competition, Julian gave that show a miss altogether or found a category to enter where the competition wasn't as fierce. It was comical at times."

"Did you ever suspect anyone of being responsible for your son's death?" asked Lydia.

"It was a case of mistaken identity," said Jenny Malone, "it had to be. Mark wouldn't hurt a fly. I knew my son. He could be ruthlessly competitive in certain areas of his life; in others, he was a passionate person who lived life to the full. The idea Mark provoked someone to the extent they chased him halfway home to fire six bullets at him is beyond belief."

"Perhaps they didn't," said Gus.

"What on earth do you mean?" asked Jenny, standing up from her chair.

"I was thinking out loud; I beg your pardon. Because of the JET petrol station incident, the police assumed that the two cars raced along Beckhampton straight at one hundred miles per hour. The 7-Series BMW overtook Mark's car, and the attack occurred as Mark slowed to enter the built-up area. The killer's car drove away after Mark lost control of his BMW and collided with parked cars. There was no CCTV evidence after the garage. There were no eyewitnesses that saw the high-speed pursuit. The other BMW may never have followed Mark towards Devizes. The argument that several people witnessed could have started and finished on the forecourt. The gunfire was followed by the sound of Mark's BMW hitting the other cars, which alerted people in the nearby properties. The only car they saw when they came outside was the stricken 5-Series BMW in the garden of a semi-detached house. Mark lay trapped inside and died later in the hospital in Swindon. Did you get there in time, Mrs Malone?"

Jenny Malone shook her head.

"How long after the accident were you notified?" asked Gus.

"I was in bed by eleven o'clock that night. I'd taken something to help me sleep. The first time I heard the door-bell chime was around a quarter past two. When they wouldn't go away, I went downstairs and answered the door. I couldn't take in what they told me; it made no sense. A car accident, maybe, as Mark drove faster than he should have more than once. The police insisted I should go with them to Swindon. We left here at ten past three and arrived in the corridor outside the emergency room in A&E at five to four. Nobody was working. The doctors and nurses just stared at the instrument monitors above Mark and one another. Then a nurse looked towards the door. Nobody needed to tell me. I saw it in her face. Mark was dead. Time of death, Three fifty-five a.m."

"I'm sorry you had to relive that dreadful experience," said Lydia, moving closer to the older woman.

"If I hadn't taken that sleeping tablet, I might have held his hand before he died. I could have told him how much I loved him. The thought of him being alone in that car as the firemen struggled to release him, knowing his life was ebbing away, haunts me every day."

Jenny Malone clung to Lydia as her tears flowed. Gus Freeman sat and watched as Lydia led Jenny Malone back to her chair.

"I'll make us a cup of tea," said Lydia and headed to the kitchen.

"I'm sorry to be such a mess. Heaven knows what you think of me. Three years, and it's still as raw as it was that first night."

"My wife, Tess, died just over three years ago from a brain aneurysm," said Gus. "She was never ill. I was in court giving evidence and found her when I got home late in the evening. There was nothing anyone could have done. But that doesn't stop me from thinking of her every single day. Mark wasn't taken from you by a sudden heart attack or an accident. That attack was deliberate. So far, we've gone with the idea that Mark argued with someone in that second BMW, and they chased and killed him. I speculated a few minutes ago that someone else wanted Mark dead. Someone who knew him well enough to learn he was driving home via Devizes, and roughly at what time."

Lydia returned from the kitchen carrying a tray with three cups, saucers, and spoons: plus a teapot, milk and sugar. Gus watched as Lydia placed the silver tray on the side table. He paused the conversation while she served the tea. How the other half lived.

"I asked myself who could have hated Mark so much that they killed him, Mr Freeman," said Jenny Malone. "The police visited me frequently. I couldn't help them identify the people at the garage. I don't think Damian could help them, either. His party was invitation-only, so he knew everyone who attended. Mark might not have met them before that night. I don't know whether they drove west to get to their homes. The motive was a mystery. It was unimaginable. After a few weeks of struggling to compre-hend it, I decided the detective who suggested Mark was mistaken for someone connected to a gang from the London area was right. It was a case of mistaken identity. It was the only logical explanation."

"I was a detective for many years before I retired four years ago, Mrs Malone," said Gus. "There were always questions that didn't get asked or answered during an inves-tigation. Sometimes those unresolved queries weren't rele-vant. Knowing the answer wouldn't have helped me find the culprit. But, as soon as I read the file on this case, a question stuck in my mind. It's kept nagging at me. I don't know whether detectives ever asked about it. So why not use the M4?"

"I don't follow," said Jenny Malone.

"How did you reach the Great Western Hospital in Marlborough Road in around forty-five minutes that night?"

"I wasn't aware of where I was half the time, but yes, I remember we drove into the city and then out towards Bathampton. Then, instead of taking the road to Chippenham, we turned left and made for the motorway. It was blue lights all the way to Swindon."

"It's forty miles, give or take, from this house to the hospital," said Gus, "even at three in the morning, it would take you twenty minutes longer via Chippenham, possibly thirty. Mark owned a powerful car and, as you said yourself, broke the speed limit occasionally. He took the scenic route in both directions that night. Why? Nobody asked that question three years ago. I want to know why someone with a high-performance car didn't use the motorway. The sixty-mile journey would have taken seventy minutes maximum. Quicker on the return trip with the foot to the floor. Mark's route was five miles shorter, a distance that was neither here nor there. But the roads aren't conducive to high speeds, so he would be lucky to make the outward journey in less than ninety minutes."

"My head's spinning with these numbers, Mr Freeman," said Jenny Malone, "why does it matter which way he drove?"

"It matters," said Gus, "because of what we read on Mark's phone."

Lydia Logan Barre gasped. Gus had asked her to read the last six records before they drove to Combe Down.

"Mark texted Damian at six-fifteen to say he was leaving his home in Marlborough Lane, guv," said Lydia. "Jenny, you called him at ten to seven to ask about Sunday lunch. You chatted for a minute as he was driving. Correct?"

"Yes, he was still in the car," said Jenny.

"Mark should have been in Newbury by seven forty-five," said Gus, "and yet he received a text from Julian Drummond at eight about Paws In The Park."

"That's the one in West Sussex in May," said Jenny, "there's another one later in the year in Kent."

"Julian wanted to know if Mark was going to West Sussex," said Lydia.

"I told you that was how they behaved," said Jenny, "did Mark reply?"

"Not for at least five minutes," said Gus, "and then he called back. Mark spoke to him directly for fifteen seconds. We don't know what they said."

"We'll check Mark's arrival time with Damian when we interview him tomorrow," said Gus, "but something doesn't add up."

"It doesn't," agreed Jenny Malone, "it's frowned upon to use your phone to call or text someone at one of Damian's parties. Mark just wouldn't have done it. He would risk not getting invited again."

"We need to speak to Damian in Newbury, to be sure," said Gus, "But where might Mark have been at eight o'clock, fifteen minutes after he should have reached the party? Answering phone calls using hands-free systems is one thing. To read a text message is both illegal and danger-ous. Mark read Julian's text within seconds of getting it, which suggests he had stopped somewhere."

"What was Mark doing that meant he could not reply for six or seven minutes?" asked Lydia.

"Why did he bother speaking with Julian?" asked Jenny, "they spent most of their time trying to avoid one another."

"Well, we've achieved something positive this afternoon, Mrs Malone," said Gus. "We know why Mark didn't use the M4 to travel to and from Newbury. He was meeting someone before the party somewhere along the route. What we have to do now is find them. I believe you can discount the mistaken identity theory, Mrs Malone. Mark knew his killer. Why Mark met that person that night, and for what reason, will explain why he died. One more thing, Mrs Malone, before we go. I never thought of pet shop managers as being top earners. Did you help your son with money? His BMW with the blacked-out windows must have set him back a tidy sum. Was it on finance, perhaps?"

"Mark never asked me for a penny towards the car. I would have given it to him gladly. When I asked if he could afford to run such an expensive car, he said not to worry. He told me you just had to know the right people."

"What do you think he meant by that?" asked Gus.

"I didn't have a clue, but I wondered if it was from the breeding business. I know nothing about it, but I've read how much the retired racehorse Frankel charges per occasion."

"I've heard the name," said Gus, "he was successful, wasn't he? What would the owner of a mare need to pay for a visit?"

"One hundred and fifty thousand pounds," said Jenny Malone.

"We're in the wrong line of business," said Gus. He stood and walked towards Jenny Malone, who remained seated.

"Thank you for your patience, Mrs Malone. I apologise if our questions made you uncomfortable. Be assured that my team and I will do everything possible to bring Mark's killer to justice. We opened a new line of enquiry today. That might well prove vital. We couldn't have done that without your help."

Jenny Malone walked with Gus to the front door. Lydia returned the tray to the kitchen and joined her boss in the hallway.

"We'll be in touch if we need anything further, " Gus said.

"I work from home, so I'm always here. Just give me a little warning that you're on your way."

Gus and Lydia returned to the car and drove into Bath.

"Follow the money," said Gus, "that's always the first thing to do in cases like this."

"I understand the economics behind obtaining a foal sired by Frankel," said Lydia. "But there can't possibly be the same sums of money available for a litter of puppies. So there must be another explanation."

"Sadly, I think that's true," said Gus.

Enigmatic as always, thought Lydia. I wonder what he's thinking.

When they reached the Old Police Station office, Luke was eager to pass on a message.

"DS Mercer called while you were out, guv. He asked if you could call as soon as you returned."

"This could be news from Honor Oak Park," said Gus, dialling Geoff's number, "Gus Freeman here. What's the latest?"

"The body in the flat fire was Ricky Gardiner," said Geoff. "The autopsy showed Gardiner suffered blunt-force trauma to the back of the head. Impossible to say whether he was dead or just unconscious when the fire started."

"Ouch," said Gus, "anything else?"

"Mike Farrell and his crew have returned to Leek Wootton. DCI Pinnock has re-assigned them to more important operations in their region."

"Understandable," said Gus, "there was nothing to gain once they learned Suzie's kidnapper was dead. They'll get the paperwork wrapped up and move on. Has the ACC, or should I say Acting Chief Constable Truelove, asked the Met to put their house in order? The buggers might listen to him now. The Met should have far better control of their undercover operatives. Whoever was Gardiner's handler wants shooting. The man had half a dozen properties on the go where he was happy to lose a few quid in rent, provided his tenants turned a blind eye to him staying the night whenever he asked. I want his bank accounts seized and his records frozen. Their forensic accountants can have a field day tracking Gardiner's dodgy receipts. Fingers crossed, Culverhouse and Plunkett will have made an error, and we'll be able to prove they paid Ricky to work for them."

"I'll chase the ACC on that," said Geoff, "you have mentioned it before. He won't have forgotten. Since his temporary promotion came through, he's been busy."

"You mean he's had less time to stare out of the window," said Gus.

"Did he ask you when you might close the Malone case?" asked Geoff.

"He did, and we're no further forward than when he asked less than four hours ago," said Gus, crossing his fingers. It was only a little white lie. They needed to check with Damian Hartley-Cole first to learn when Mark arrived at the party. If Gus was correct, then the money for the customised BMW held the clue to his murder.

"I'll let you get on," said Geoff. "I'm not sure yet what he's up to, but our temporary Chief Constable is meeting Peter Morgan first thing tomorrow morning. I'm to forget our regular ten o'clock meeting. Still, it gives me a chance to catch up on other matters. DC Blessing Umeh, for instance. I'm negotiating with DI Andy Carlton to agree on a date for her transfer. If he sees things my way, Blessing will join you on Monday, the second of July."

"We might have finished this Malone case by then," said Gus. "But if the Met are still dragging their heels following the Gardiner money, the young lady will find I'm on my allotment in Urchfont enjoying a proper retirement."

Geoff Mercer laughed.

"You love it too much to walk away, Gus," he said, "Kenneth has four more cold cases that need your expert attention. If he puts his mind to it, now he's gained a boost to his ego, Kenneth might squeeze a couple more unsolved murders into your stay with the CRT before he retires. We can't disappoint him."

"You're all heart," said Gus, "right, this Malone case won't solve itself. Cheers."

When Gus ended the call, Luke Sherman walked to Gus's desk and sat beside him.

"Yes, Luke? This looks serious."

"I need to tell you something, guv. I called Nicky as soon as you left for Combe Down with Lydia. Nicky and I have been together for six years. I mentioned on Monday that he's older than me. Nicky was twenty-four when we met, and he'd been out for five years."

"I can see you find this difficult, Luke," said Gus, "don't worry. Just cut to the chase. You told me you didn't know

Mark Malone. Did Nicky meet Mark before you got together?"

"No, guv," said Luke, "it was Patrick Boddington. Nicky looked to Patrick as a mentor when he first started visiting bars and clubs in Bath. Nicky became besotted with him. He laughs about it now and realises that it meant nothing to Patrick, although he learned a lot. Nicky changed jobs and lived in Salisbury for a year after they split up. When Nicky returned to Bath one weekend, he spotted Patrick in a bar with someone who looked suspiciously young. The next time he looked across, the pair had disappeared. We met two years later, and it's been a monogamous relationship since that night."

"Thank you for being honest," said Gus, "do you think Boddington could have anything to do with Malone's death?"

"What about the phone calls either side of midnight, guv?" said Luke. "Boddington could have been the last person to speak to Mark before he died. We can't ignore that. Should I stand aside from the case, guv?"

"Not a chance, Luke," said Gus, "I'll take Lydia with me tomorrow to speak with Damian Hartley-Cole, but before I go, what can you tell me about these parties Damian held? Jenny Malone said I would never have attended one like it. I nodded as if I knew what she was talking about."

"We haven't talked to Damian yet, but we can assume it was a sex party. All parties are different. The murder file indicated there were no more than six people in the house that night. When the emergency services released Mark Malone from the car, he wore street clothes. There was a record of items in a drawstring bag in the boot."

"Anything I would recognise?" asked Gus.

"A jockstrap and harness, lube, condoms, bottled water.

A change of clothes and trainers. No party drugs of any kind."

"Jenny Malone told us that Mark was a passionate young man who lived life to the full. When I was your age, I drank three beers before going to the local dance and, if there was a bar, had another beer to pluck up enough courage to ask a girl to dance. You must think that is very tame by comparison. Oh, and if I got an invitation to a party, there was always cake with candles, and if the grown-ups left us alone for thirty minutes, a game of spin the bottle. A kiss without tongues was a real result. Taking even one condom would have been reckless in the extreme."

Luke couldn't help laughing.

"Look, not every gay man is the same as Mark. The same as not everyone who attended parties after the war went home only having kissed someone."

"Hang on, what do you mean, after the war? My first party that included games in the dark with girls was in 1970."

"Almost fifty years ago then, guv. At the start of the decade fashion forgot."

"I can't argue with that remark, Luke. Anyway, I'm better prepared for tomorrow's interview now. I'll brief Lydia on the answers we need and let her take the lead. I don't want to show my ignorance any more than necessary."

"I know you'll want to update the Freeman Files with the conversation you had with Jenny Malone," said Luke, "but can you share the highlights?"

"The timeline of the journey and the phone records don't appear to match," said Gus, "Mark should have arrived in Newbury well before eight o'clock. Unless Damian shoots my theory out of the water in the morning,

Mark stopped somewhere between Bath and Newbury. I told Lydia we needed to follow the money. It's often the simplest way. Mark had loads of cash to buy his BMW without asking his mother, Jenny, for a handout. Where did he get that money? Mark may have planned to stop on the way home, which explains his chosen route."

"Do you think it was drugs, guv?" asked Luke, "Mark carried no drugs in the car, and he was clean according to the autopsy report."

"The best way to make money from drugs is to avoid sampling the product, Luke," said Gus, "I fear we still have more to learn about the late Mark Malone. Sadly, his mother is a lovely lady and whatever we discover is likely to shatter the image she had of her only child. Sometimes, I hate this job."

Luke returned to his desk. Lydia continued to update her copy of the Freeman Files. Gus looked at the clock. Time to get home. Tomorrow was another day.

Chapter Six

A WEDNESDAY EVENING chez Freeman these days could be fun.

He'd entertained Vera Jennings and Suzie Ferris in the past few months, although not on the same evening. He'd returned to find signs of an intruder on one occasion where an Albanian gangster left a threatening message. A warning that led to an incident that wasn't a barrel of laughs, and he'd been lucky to escape with his life.

Gus had always imagined that variety had been plentiful when he and Tess lived in the bungalow while she was alive. There was something to discuss, places to go, people to see, wasn't there? Had that been true, though, looking back? Or was it familiarity? Would their lives have become a tedious repetition of the same bland experiences as they grew old together?

The three years after Tess died sadly lacked any variety or excitement. Gus was on a different treadmill: - gardening, reading, drinking and sleeping. But, again, loneliness was an issue he kept at bay to a degree by gardening, reading, and drinking.

Which did he prefer? The constant calm waters before Kenneth Truelove's phone call asking him to return to work, or the hustle and bustle of recent months?

Gus reckoned that today was a great example of how his life had changed.

The conversations with Luke Sherman and Jenny Malone touched on areas he'd never faced. He was an innocent abroad. Sometimes when he spoke with Lydia Logan Barre, he felt totally out of touch with younger people and what they did in their leisure time.

This afternoon, Jenny Malone called her ex-husband a bigot. Yet when Jenny asked Lydia where she came from, it was clear she wasn't expecting the answer Lydia gave. To her credit, Lydia didn't react despite probably having to deal with racial stereotyping every day of her life.

As Luke said, it takes all sorts.

On this Wednesday evening, Gus drove through Devizes to Urchfont and straight to the bungalow. He'd ignored his kitchen for too long, and it was time to assess the damage. Gus spent an hour checking the contents of the fridge and his two freezers. He soon had a list of fresh items required from the supermarket, plus a series of menus designed to eliminate the older stocks hidden at the back of shelves and in corners.

All the while, he thought of Dominic Culverhouse and that preliminary meeting coming up on Friday at Portishead. Did Culverhouse kill Ricky Gardiner? How would he handle Sandra Plunkett's suicide? Could he turn it to his advantage in any way?

The phone ringing in the hallway interrupted his thoughts. It was Neil Davis.

"Hello, Neil," said Gus, "good to hear your voice again."

"You too, guv," said Neil, "I wanted to tell you I'll be back at work on Monday."

"That's terrific news, Neil. How are you both?"

"I'm fine, guv," said Neil, "there's been plenty to deal with, not just losing the baby, but dealing with my Dad's affairs, both here and in Spain. It will take time to complete. My mother's coping with most of the paperwork. So, I feel ready to get back to work. It will take my mind off everything else that's happening."

"I understand, Neil. How's Melody?" asked Gus.

Neil paused.

"She's staying at her mother's next week, guv, rather than be alone in the house while I'm working. Her Mum's happy to look after her. After the funeral, we had a quiet word, and Melody's mother suggested I get back to normal. She'll try to bring Melody out of her depressed state without running to the doctor for pills."

"I hope things go well with everything, Neil. You've had a lot to withstand. Being selfish, I'll be glad to have you back with the team. I've missed your input. Luke will stay with us. I don't remember how things stood the last time we spoke. Forget that for now. We'll have a proper catch-up on Monday."

"Okay, guv, I'll see you then."

With that, Neil rang off, and Gus returned to the kitchen. Time to try one of those menus.

As he polished off a mushroom risotto, his thoughts, this time about the Mark Malone case, had to wait. The phone rang again.

"Hi, Gus," It was Suzie Ferris.

"Hello, you," said Gus, "how was your first day?"

"Half-day," Suzie corrected him.

"You can't kid a kidder, Suzie. I heard you crept along the corridor towards Geoff's office before your official start time."

"Kassie Trotter, I presume?" said Suzie.

"She doesn't miss much," said Gus, "I'm sorry that you won't get your chance to watch Ricky Gardiner get jailed for your kidnapping."

"There are loads of rumours flying around at London Road," said Suzie.

"Tell them to mind their own business," said Gus.

"Not you and me, silly. I mean the Chief Constable and ACC Culverhouse, for one, and how Ricky Gardiner died, for another. You only have to take two days off, and the world turns upside down. Geoff updated me just before lunchtime on Sandra Plunkett and her partner. I can't forgive Sandra for her part in my kidnapping, but I wouldn't wish her dead. As for Culverhouse, well, we know what a devious swine he was when he worked here. It wasn't only Terry Davis that he dropped in it. As I was coming through the ranks, I heard stories about him. He's flown too close to the sun for the last time."

"Don't count on him crashing and burning yet, Suzie. He's devious, all right. Did Geoff Mercer update you on the news from the autopsy on Gardiner?"

"No, I missed that. What did it show?"

"It was Gardiner, as we suspected. Someone bashed him over the head before setting the fire. My guess is it was Culverhouse. There has to be evidence somewhere. I hope the Met don't miss it. Last Friday, the man got suspended from Portishead, pending investigation. On Monday, he turns up at Greenwich to work for his buddy from Bramshill. How far was his new posting from Ricky

Gardiner? Five miles, I ask you. How could anyone not see that was suspicious?"

"He *was* entitled to a transfer," said Suzie. "By the way, are you busy this weekend?"

"I don't intend to let work get in the way," said Gus, "we've got several interviews to get through tomorrow and Friday. First up in the morning is one Damian Hartley-Cole, from Newbury, an interior designer by day and a sex party organiser at night."

"Really? Listen and learn, Gus. I'm looking forward to the weekend even more now."

After Suzie rang off, Gus checked the spare keys were still in his jacket pocket. He placed them on the worktop in the kitchen, next to the cafetiere, just in case.

There were no more calls. When Gus wandered from the lounge to the bedroom at ten-thirty, he spotted a note hanging from the letterbox. It must have been there when he got home from work, but he'd missed it.

Gus didn't recognise the handwriting.

'Gus, I didn't see Bert yesterday nor today at the allotment. I popped around to check if he was ill, but he'd received terrible news from Canada. I'll call on you tomorrow evening, if I may, to tell you face-to-face. Clemency.'

Wednesday evenings can be fun, Gus thought. Tonight had been uneventful until now. Poor Bert. What on earth happened?

Thursday, 7 June 2018

GUS ARRIVED at the Old Police Station a few minutes before nine o'clock. Lydia's Mini sat in its usual spot. Good, thought Gus, we might complete a round trip today. A journey that took in the delights of Newbury and Milton Keynes.

Upstairs in the office, Luke and Lydia were deep in discussion.

"When you're ready, Lydia," said Gus, "I need you to drive today."

"Sorry, guv," she replied, "I was just updating Luke on Alex."

"Tell me in the car," said Gus, "I want to hear how he's progressing."

Lydia grabbed her things and headed for the lift.

"Luke, I had a call from Neil last night," said Gus, "he's returning to work on Monday."

"Terrific, guv," said Luke. "Was there something you wanted me to discover while you're gone?"

"Provided Damian's interview doesn't last the day, I'm hoping to get to Milton Keynes to talk to Julian Drummond. Why don't you drive to Bath for a chat with Patrick Boddington?"

Luke nodded, although Gus thought he looked less than pleased with his mission.

Gus lowered himself into Lydia's car and prepared for a scary ride to Newbury. First, he risked one eye while they negotiated traffic on the bypass. Then, he opened both eyes and relaxed as they left Chippenham to drive towards the M4. Traffic was steady this morning, not enough to delay them but sufficient to stop Lydia from driving like a madwoman.

"I told you Alex had started his detox, didn't I guv?" asked Lydia.

"I caught the headlines but not the gory details," said Gus.

"You sent him home on the twenty-second, guv. I persuaded him to get help. Alex had a pre-assessment to determine his individual detox needs. After Terry Davis's funeral, we went back to his place. The clinic contacted him on Friday morning. He started his detox on Saturday. Alex had to stay at the clinic for six nights. They gradually reduced the dosage daily and gave him other medication to help with nausea and vomiting. When I see him tomorrow, the detox stage should be complete. Then he goes into the rehab stage. He knows we'll be there for him to make sure he doesn't relapse. Alex told me on the phone last night that he's aiming for Monday the second of July."

"That would be a blessing," said Gus, "but we may need to ask Geoff Mercer for additional furniture and more coffee mugs."

Lydia had to stop wondering what that meant because Gus then briefed her on which questions he wanted her to ask when they reached Newbury. On Andover Road, she found Wood Ridge, and they parked her Mini outside the Hartley-Cole residence at ten-thirty-three. Gus saw the curtain twitch in the living room.

"There's someone at home," he said.

"Damian is expecting us," said Lydia.

"Good luck, Lydia," said Gus, "I'll introduce us, and then you're on your own."

Damian Hartley-Cole answered the doorbell.

Gus had expected something flamboyant, which only emphasised how little he knew. But instead, the tall, slender man who stood before them looked ordinary in a

V-neck sweater, shirt, slacks and trainers. He was an interior designer who seemed more like a golfer than that camp presenter from Changing Rooms. Unfortunately, Gus couldn't recall the name now. Tess had watched the series avidly, but Gus used the time to catch up on paperwork.

"Come in," said Damian, "oh, thank goodness you didn't turn up in a police car. My neighbours would have an attack of the vapours. Straight through to the kitchen. I can carry on cooking and chatting with you. Do you both want a coffee? I'm drinking a glass of wine, but you're on duty. Sorry, I'm rambling. I'm a bag of nerves, and I did nothing wrong."

"I wondered when you would ever take a breath," said Gus.

"We both drink our coffee black," said Lydia, "one sugar in mine."

Damian nodded and set to work.

"There's nothing to alarm you," said Gus. "As my colleague explained when he called, we're taking a fresh look at Mark Malone's murder. I'm Gus Freeman, a consultant with Wiltshire Police. Lydia Logan Barre is my colleague, and she will tell you what we need to learn about what happened in the hours leading up to Mark's death."

Damian placed two coffees on the kitchen table. He took a generous swig from his large glass of white wine and turned his attention to the pans on the professional-looking hob.

"Is that a Rangemaster?" asked Lydia.

"Mmm," said Damian, "when you entertain as much as I do, darling, you need the best. So, what do you need to know?"

"How long had you known Mark?" asked Lydia.

"Two years, maybe three. We met through a mutual friend."

"Someone from Bath, perhaps?"

"No, he came from Brighton, I believe; he's moved on now. Lives in Tenerife with a Brazilian dancer."

"Did you know Mark well," asked Lydia.

"Intimately," Damian replied, "but we weren't exclusive."

"What can you tell us about the party here that night?"

"Very little, I'm afraid," said Damian. "There were five guests. Mark drove here from Bath. The others came from Reading, Tottenham, Esher, and Sittingbourne. That's all I'm prepared to divulge because my guest list is privileged information. I would lose hundreds of contacts overnight if I disclosed their details. Marriages and relationships could be at stake. Confidentiality is everything."

"What time did Mark get here?" asked Lydia.

"We had agreed to meet at nine," said Damian, topping up his wine glass.

"Could you answer the question please, Sir," said Gus.

"Mark didn't get here until half-past."

"Did any of your guests drive a 7-Series BMW?" asked Gus.

"Heavens, no," said Damian, "I recall a Welsh detective asked me that question. Why on earth they thought that car had anything to do with us, I can't imagine?"

"DI Trefor Davies asked you about it, did he?" asked Gus.

"It may have been someone with that name. But I didn't like the man. He was too judgmental."

"When the party ended, did you see whether anyone drove away from the house in the same direction as Mark?" asked Lydia.

"Who told you the party ended? Mark was late arriving and left early. We were still going until the sun came up, darling. Nobody followed Mark from here. Unless someone was waiting for him out on Andover Road."

"Mark texted you when he was leaving Bath," said Lydia, "were you surprised that he left home as early as a quarter past six?"

"Mark was Mark," said Damian, "why was he late? Why did he leave early? Who knows? When he was in a good mood which was often, he was the life and soul of any occasion. That night he had something on his mind."

"Did he talk about it?" asked Lydia. "You were close, Damian. Would he have shared something with you if it troubled him?"

"Two years earlier, when we first met, maybe. Not towards the end. We saw each other less frequently over the twelve months before Mark died. However, he always had an invitation to my parties, and he attended others across the south of the country where we met up to gossip. Mark hadn't fallen out of favour with anyone we both knew, as far as I was aware."

"Are you implying Mark fell out with someone, but you only found out after he died?" asked Lydia.

"I don't tell tales," said Damian, "if this gets back to the person involved, it could cause problems."

"A young man died," said Gus, "in case you need reminding. If you have any information to help us find Mark's killer, I suggest you tell us everything you know."

"I told you that anyone could have followed Mark to that JET garage outside Marlborough if someone was waiting on the main road. One of our circle of friends lives in a village outside Salisbury. There is only one road through the village. A few months before Mark died, there was a party at our friend's house. Well, it's more of a mansion than a house, surrounded by eleven acres of country park. A six-foot-high wall surrounds the estate. It must have kept the dry-stone walling brigade in work for months back in the eighteenth century when they built it. The gates are closed after you enter, so every nosy villager can see anyone parked outside in the narrow lane. A black SUV stayed outside from dusk to dawn. Can you believe it? Our friend received a dozen or more complaints from the locals. Our host asked us if that SUV had anything to do with us. Everyone denied it. After Mark's death, our Salisbury friend confided in me he'd crossed Mark's name off his contact list. One of his neighbours had told him the SUV only drove away once a BMW with tinted windows came through the gates."

Lydia glanced towards Gus. Was that significant? Who could have been driving the black SUV?

"We might need to contact you again, Mr Hartley-Cole," said Gus. "Call us if you've omitted to tell us something useful for our investigation. I know you wish to protect confidentiality over events behind closed doors, but our job is to solve murders. So I've never shrunk from ruffling a few feathers to get the answers I want."

"You know best," said Damian, "but honestly, I don't think anyone here that night had a hand in Mark's murder."

Gus and Lydia made their way outside to the Mini. Damian closed the front door behind them.

"What was your impression?" asked Gus.

"A lovely kitchen," said Lydia, "but he made sure we didn't see inside any of the other rooms, didn't he?"

"None of our business, Lydia," said Gus, "they're all consenting adults. So who are we to pass judgement? Do you think Damian was right that the murder had nothing to do with the party?"

"Yes, guv," said Lydia. "The earlier party in Salisbury was the clincher for me. Whoever was in that black SUV waited for Mark to appear. We can't say whether he was supposed to leave the party earlier from Damian's, but whatever the people in that SUV wanted, it was important enough to wait for ten hours until they could follow him. Damian was adamant that nobody drove the 7-Series BMW to *any* of their parties. Was the argument with the driver of the BMW a spot of road rage between Newbury and the Beckhampton roundabout, as someone suggested at the time? What if Mark tried to get away from the black SUV and cut up the BMW?"

"We don't have any proof there was ever a black SUV on that road, Lydia," said Gus, "yours is not a fanciful idea, but it is conjecture. If only we had more eyewitness accounts, CCTV evidence, something to show there were other vehicles at the scene driven by people who knew Mark Malone."

"Shall I drive us to Milton Keynes now, guv? To meet Julian Shih Tzu?"

"What time is it now? Half-past eleven. We'll go via Oxford to avoid the boredom of motorway driving. You should still get us there by one o'clock.

"You think I drove too fast on the way here then?" said Lydia, "I imagine the A34 will curtail my girlish enthusiasm for speed."

"We live in hope," said Gus, checking his seat belt.

Gus was right. Lydia drew up outside the terraced property belonging to Julian Drummond at five minutes to one.

"A modest residence," said Gus, "for a photographer. I wonder if he has a studio somewhere in town?"

"I didn't check what he photographed, guv," said Lydia, "so I don't know about a studio. Did you automatically assume it was people and think he majored in glamour models?"

"Dogs," replied Gus.

"That's not fair, guv. I expect some are nice young things."

"No. Dogs will be what Julian photographs. Either at the dog shows he's so fond of or in the owner's loving arms."

"You're not a dog person, are you?"

"I'm not an animal person, Lydia. It's not compulsory, thank goodness. I lost count of the number of criminals I arrested, where there were many pets around the home. If you asked why they resorted to theft, the standard reply was that they didn't have enough money to put food on the table. I tripped over the dogs and cats as I took them out of the living room, kicked the empties in the hallway, and stepped over the cigarette butts on the step outside the door. The penny never dropped that I did it deliberately, trying to make them realise the solution to their economic woes stared them in the face."

"I don't know whether to take you seriously sometimes, guv," said Lydia, "surely, your heart goes out to a little puppy?"

Gus turned his head to see what had caught Lydia's eye. Julian Drummond stood on his front doorstep with a King Charles Spaniel in his arms.

"The poor thing must have lost the use of its legs," said Gus. "Come on, let's get this over with."

Julian took two steps back as Lydia and Gus reached the door.

"Have you come for me?" he said,

"We came to talk to you, Mr Drummond," said Gus. "You haven't committed an offence, have you?"

Julian Drummond shook his head vigorously.

The fashion police might disagree, Lydia thought. Julian's shiny blue suit reminded her of a cheesy game show host from the Seventies. Not that Lydia was alive to watch them when they first aired, but it was difficult to stop her mother from watching re-runs on one of the satellite TV channels.

"You want to come in, I suppose," said Julian, "the front room's the tidiest place. Mitzi has run wild in the rest of the downstairs rooms, I'm afraid."

Gus watched the forty-three-year-old photographer picking his way gingerly through the clutter of furniture in the living room. There was hardly a square foot of carpet anywhere. He'd never been in a place so crammed with furniture and rubbish.

Old newspapers, magazines, books, and photo albums covered several side tables. Two display cabinets held photos, figurines, and carvings of dogs, plus an assortment of trophies. The layer of dust suggested it was too much hassle to remove items to clean and polish the wooden surfaces.

"If you can find a seat," said Julian. He stood in front of the fireplace with Mitzi still staring at Gus from his owner's armpit.

Gus and Lydia did their best. Gus fetched a chair from the dining room next door. There was nothing on it, and Gus wondered what it had done to get left out. He sat and nodded to Lydia.

Lydia explained to Julian who they both were and reminded him why they were there.

"I'll help if I can," said Julian, "Mark and I had our differences, but they're not important now."

"When was the last time you spoke with Mark?" asked Lydia.

"Just after eight o'clock that Saturday evening," said Julian, stroking Mitzi.

"You texted Mark ten to fifteen minutes earlier," said Lydia, looking at her notes. "Should I remind you what you wrote?"

"I asked Mark if he was going to the West Sussex Paws In The Park at the end of the month."

"Did you know he was driving to Newbury for a party?" asked Lydia.

"We didn't socialise," said Julian. "Mark and I didn't move in the same circles if you follow me."

"Are you married or in a relationship?" asked Lydia.

"Do you think a woman would want to live here? No, my life has always centred around my dogs. My parents got me interested in the business from a young age. Dog owners and people interested in dogs go to events for many reasons. Some learn about unique dog breeds, and others show off their dog's talents in competitions. They took me to different dog events across the country, from small local events to huge shows attracting thousands of people. My father died in the front bedroom, directly above us, when I was fourteen. He was fifty-two. My mother got up to make a cup of tea and took it upstairs with the morning paper. I watched the paperboy smoking a crafty fag as he cycled up the street. Next, I heard the cup hitting the floor and Mum screaming."

Gus tried to remember whether this was a question he'd had on the list he suggested Lydia used. But, unfortunately, it wasn't getting them closer to finding Mark's killer.

"When did you lose your mother?" asked Gus.

"Two years ago," said Julian. Mitzi wriggled in his arms and stretched to lick her master's cheek.

"How did Mark reply to your text message, and what did he say?" asked Gus.

"He called me to say he was giving the show a miss that year," said Julian.

"I imagine you were relieved," said Lydia, "less competition for you."

"It's not all about winning, you know. Mark thought so. But for many of us, it's meeting other dog owners and learning about canine behaviour. The dogs enjoy the events too. It helps them keep well socialised."

"Was it usual for Mark to call you, or did you keep in contact by text or email?" asked Gus.

Julian thought for a moment.

"Do you know, I think that was one of only a handful of occasions when we spoke on the phone. I suppose I'd known Mark for ten years, and we bumped into one another during at least ten shows each year."

"Why didn't he ignore your text or reply in kind?" asked Gus.

"How do I know?" replied Julian.

"Mark was heading for Newbury that evening," said Lydia, "but when your text arrived, he must have stopped somewhere. Do you know who he might visit on the road between Bath and Newbury?"

"I didn't know any of Mark's gay friends," said Julian, "but there could be dozens of dog owners and breeders along that route. I can't think of anyone Mark knew, especially well, off the top of my head. I could check the details of the local shows to see if a name rings a bell. They could have been discussing a breeding partnership. I wouldn't have a clue. So why is it important?"

"We don't know that it is, Sir," said Gus. "Mark Malone took over three hours to reach the party in Newbury. Anyone could cover that distance in ninety minutes without busting a gut, which suggests he stopped for a considerable length of time."

"While he was wherever he was," said Lydia, "doing whatever he was doing, he read your text, waited six or seven minutes, and then called you."

Julian and Mitzi both stared at Lydia open-mouthed.

"I think my colleague wanted to say, can you remember the exact words Mark used during that call?" said Gus.

"I'll be giving it a miss this year, darling. Ring me on Monday," said Julian.

"Didn't that seem out of character, Sir?" asked Gus. "You were at each other's throats most of the time, according to Mark's mother. You just told us the phone call was one of only a handful in the ten years you'd known one another."

"I thought it odd for Mark to ask me to call him. It certainly wasn't normal."

"You didn't mention this phone call during the original investigation?" asked Gus.

"I don't think anyone asked me to repeat it, word for word. I only said that Mark told me he wasn't going to Paws In The Park that May. Nobody followed up on the conversation after that."

"What car do you drive, Sir?" asked Gus.

"I have a VW camper van from the Seventies," said Julian. "I need the space for the dogs and the camera equipment. Also, it's expensive to spend a weekend away. So I sleep in the van to save money."

"There's not much money in the dog show business, then?" asked Gus.

"Crufts is the biggest dog show in the world, so we plan our build-up to the main event every year. Of course, everyone wants to receive the ultimate prize, but the prestige, not the two hundred pounds, is what's important."

"Two hundred quid for the top dog?" asked Gus, "how did Mark Malone get to drive around in a fancy car? Did that money come from breeding? How much a year could you earn from your Shih Tzu?"

Julian Drummond looked puzzled.

"I don't know where you got the impression I was interested in breeds other than King Charles Spaniels," he replied. "That was what Mum and Dad always had. So I carried on with the same breed in their memory. As for making money from breeding, I break even at best."

"So, the competition money is minimal, and breeding is more for the love of the animals than for profit," said Gus, trying to make sense of things.

"Exactly," said Julian.

"Do you have a full-time job, Sir?" asked Gus.

"How do I earn a living?" asked Julian. "Through my photography, of course. I attend dozens of shows. Take the Heart of England show in Daventry, for instance, with eighteen novelties and four pedigree classes. Everyone wants their dog's photo taken. There's even a photo competition. I don't drink or smoke, and as you can see, I live alone. My only extravagance is the clothing I wear to shows. The old suit I'm wearing is one I've relegated to day-to-day wear. I have a wardrobe full of them in different colours. It's how customers pick me out in the crowds when they want their photo taken."

"Thank you for your time today, Mr Drummond," said

Gus. "If you could provide that list of possible dog owners or breeders that Mark Malone might have visited on the night he died, we'd be very pleased to receive it."

"I'll start work on it straight away, Mr Freeman," said Julian, "good afternoon to you both."

Lydia and Gus walked to the car. Julian raised a hand, and Mitzi barked as the front door closed.

"That was awkward," said Lydia, "we thought the Julian Shih Tzu in Mark's contact list referred to the dogs he bred and showed."

"Mark Malone had a wicked sense of humour, Lydia," said Gus, "but his spelling wasn't great."

Chapter Seven

LYDIA PULLED AWAY from the kerb, and they were soon heading towards the motorway in her Mini.

"If I get to the nearest M4 junction, we should arrive back at the Old Police Station in two hours, give or take, guv," she said.

"There's no rush, young lady," said Gus, "Luke has gone to Bath to search out Patrick Boddington. It would have been a decent day if he had learned as much from him as we did from our two witnesses. We can run through what we've learned and then come back fresh in the morning."

"What did you make of the phone call, guv," asked Lydia, "I could see you took more interest in matters when Julian gave us the exact wording."

"Well, you asked questions that gave him free rein to tell us his life story. I could have done without that."

"Sorry, guv. I wanted to get Julian to relax. I sensed he was nervous. I felt sorry for Mitzi because Julian was hanging onto her for grim death."

"That phone call from Mark was out of character," said Gus. "So, what lay behind the words he used?"

"Ah, I see what you're driving at, guv. Wherever Mark was, he couldn't speak openly. He tried to pass Julian a message because he was in danger. Mark referred to Julian as darling and asked him to ring on Monday, which he would never do."

"Julian didn't realise Mark was trying to tell him he was in trouble. What Julian could have done, I don't know. But Mark must have stopped at someone's house on the way to Newbury. Either that, or he got stopped by someone and taken to a house. If only we could identify the town or the address."

"Let's hope Julian can think of the right owners and breeders, guv," said Lydia, "we could have a lot of people to trace and interview."

"If that's where the culprit lies. I might run through the detailed phone records you got from the Hub," said Gus. "We gleaned useful information from only a handful of calls and messages. Let's hope the key to this murder lies in those records somewhere."

"You must analyse any name tags carefully, guv," said Lydia. "If there was a Doug Butcher among Mark's friends, he could be a serial killer, not the guy who got Mark his lamb shanks."

"Very droll. If Mark were more sensible, Doug Butcher would be a real person," said Gus. "Maybe people need to disguise their contacts from their partners; I wouldn't know. Do you keep your mobile phone out of Alex's reach? Do you have a password to restrict access if you lose it?"

"You only do things like that if you have something to hide, guv, surely?" said Lydia. "OK, I would worry if I *lost* my phone because even though I locked it, a hacker could get into it in seconds. But, with Alex, I leave it lying around without fretting that he might sneak a quick look to see who I've been calling. You must have trust in a relationship."

"I wasn't thinking of you and Alex in particular, Lydia," said Gus. "I suppose the parties Mark attended made me wonder how valuable the information on his phone could be."

"I'm not sure I follow," said Lydia.

"Damian was a friend," said Gus, "and although Damian invited those other four men from the Home Counties, there's no suggestion Mark had ever met any of them. I imagine the thrill of sex with strangers attracted Mark and the others in the first place. Luke told me the drawstring bag in the boot was significant. The bag contained clothing and other essentials. Once the party was in full swing, it also provided a semi-secure place for items they didn't want to carry around, such as a phone or an expensive watch. If I was in a similar situation, I might leave my valuables somewhere safe in the car or not take them with me if they got nicked. One of Damian's friends could be a blackmailer, using data from the phone to extract money for Mark's silence."

"Do you think that might have happened at another party, guv?" asked Lydia, "someone got hold of Mark's phone, and they drove the black SUV. That person put the squeeze on Mark for money."

"It's another theory with no supporting evidence, I'm afraid," said Gus.

"There is another reason for Mark to keep a phone handy, guv," said Lydia, "what if something went wrong at a party, and he needed to call for help?"

"Things could get awkward, I guess," said Gus.

"No risk, no reward, I suppose," said Lydia.

They sat silently for the next minute as Lydia eased her way from the outside lane as the Chippenham junction loomed. Then, when she was in position, she continued.

"I don't believe anything in Mark's phone gave him cause for concern. Remember the breakdown I read out to you—forty per cent of his contacts aligned with the pet shop business. Twenty per cent were people similar to Julian Drummond on the dog show circuit. The rest was family and friends, every one of whom knew Mark was gay. So there was little scope for a blackmailer."

"I think you might have unwittingly stumbled onto something," said Gus.

"Mark had a burner phone, you mean," said Lydia.

"How long have you been sitting on that idea?"

"I had a lightbulb moment when you mentioned how you might behave at one of Damian's parties. Before Mark got to Wood Ridge, something or someone scared him. You asked me to read the last half-dozen messages on the night Mark died. I scanned the page out of interest and saw nothing unusual. Pet food suppliers, advertising for the Bath Chronicle, birthday greetings for a friend called Sacha. If Mark got involved in criminal activity, there was no sign of it on his phone."

"So, we need to dig deeper to find out what happened to his other phone. Was it in the car the night he died? Did his killer retrieve it before fleeing the scene?"

"Was it essential Mark had it with him that night, guv?" asked Lydia, "Could he have pre-arranged the eight o'clock meeting with the mysterious SUV driver? He might have left it at home if he didn't want to risk losing his phone at the party. Did the police find one when they searched his flat in Marlborough Lane?"

"There was no mention of it in the murder file," said

Gus, "I wish we had followed this line of thinking earlier. I would have told Luke to ask Patrick Boddington if he still had a key to Mark's apartment."

"They weren't an item any longer, guv. Jenny Malone told us the relationship was purely platonic by that time."

"Mark didn't confide in his mother too often. I would describe their relationship as being at arm's length. I doubt if she had access to his apartment. However, Mark viewed Patrick as a mentor, and they occasionally met up for a meal. We'll see evidence of that in Mark's phone, plus we could check his bank accounts. That's a job for Luke tomorrow. He can follow the money to see when and where the money for this BMW started appearing. With our luck, that will be as elusive as proving Ricky Gardiner got paid to kill Terry Davis."

"If it came from a criminal enterprise, it would more likely have been cash though, guv, wouldn't it?" asked Lydia.

"Either cash or a complicated spider's web of transactions designed to make an accountant's head spin."

Lydia waited for Gus to continue, but he was deep in thought. She wondered if he'd notice a slight increase in speed as they rattled along towards Junction 17. Twenty minutes later, she pulled into the car park below the Old Police Station office. Luke's car wasn't there yet.

"Patrick Boddington must have had plenty to say, guv," said Lydia.

"Luke may have followed your approach and invited Patrick to tell him his life story," said Gus, "in which case we'll be waiting for him all evening. I rarely ask this, but would you mind making me a coffee?"

"Of course not, guv," said Lydia. She dropped her things on her desk and went to the restroom. Gus heard the Gaggia fire up and waited patiently for Lydia to return.

"There we are, guv. One black coffee without sugar. Thirsty, were you?"

"Not at all. I needed something to steady my nerves after you overtook that tractor when we neared Chippenham Golf Club."

"You were away with the fairies. I didn't think you noticed," said Lydia. "I had plenty of room."

"You may have had plenty of room on your side. I practically sat in the cab with the tractor driver."

The twinkle in her boss's eye told Lydia it was another gentle leg pull. She returned to her desk and drank her cup of coffee. Then, finally, they both heard the lift descend to the ground floor.

"The wanderer returns," said Gus.

Luke Sherman strolled into the office.

"Oh, you're back. How did it go?" Luke asked.

"We were here first," said Gus, "we'll ask the questions."

"Patrick Boddington reminded me of Quentin Crisp, guv," said Luke, "did you ever see The Naked Civil Servant?"

"On one of my earlier cases, yes, Luke. I was on patrol in a Panda car in the countryside on the edge of Salisbury Plain. The gentleman in question was on the back seat of a Rolls Royce with an adolescent farm girl."

"I think we've got crossed wires, guv," said Luke.

"More than likely, Luke. Let's leave Patrick's appearance until later. I want to know what they said during the two phone calls he shared with Mark Malone on either side of midnight."

"Patrick couldn't recall, guv," said Luke.

"Rubbish," said Gus, "Jenny Malone remembered every

word. As she said, it was the last time they spoke. She received that call six hours before Mark died. Neighbours heard the gunshots at around twelve thirty-five, a mere thirty minutes after Patrick and Mark conducted a seven-minute conversation."

"Patrick Boddington is hiding something, guv," said Lydia.

"Did he have a key to Mark's apartment in Marlborough Lane?" asked Gus.

"I didn't ask, guv. There wasn't any suggestion that anyone other than Mark had a key in the murder file. So what are you driving at?"

"Lydia and I will update the Freeman Files before we leave tonight," said Gus. "I suggest you do the same. Tomorrow morning we'll try to create a meaningful cast of characters and actions for the night Mark died. There are several unanswered questions, and Patrick Boddington may hold the key to several of them. So before you go home tonight, Luke, phone Boddington and tell him we need to speak with him again. Don't get fobbed off with excuses. We'll call Manvers Street and borrow an interview room if he gets obstructive. Boddington spends his life spinning stories to vulnerable and impressionable young men. I suspect he thought he could deceive you too, Luke. He'll have me to face tomorrow, under caution, if necessary."

"Yes, guv," said Luke.

Gus, Luke, and Lydia were hard at work for the rest of the afternoon updating the Freeman Files. At five o'clock, Gus watched the others leave and sat in the office pondering what the day had delivered. What could Mark Malone have been doing that cost him his life? Perhaps it wasn't a surprise his mother was unaware of anything suspicious. They weren't close. People like Damian Hartley-Cole and

Julian Drummond were acquaintances, not Mark's bosom buddies. Lydia stressed that his mobile phone held nothing out of the ordinary. Gus checked the files for the detailed breakdown that the Hub had provided.

Lydia was right. None of the contacts felt out of place, and the pet shop contacts were what you would expect. Mark's link to the dog show world was more colourful, but even there, the phone numbers were for event organisers, fellow owners, and a handful of breeders.

Gus wondered if he'd ever had eighty friends during his lifetime. His home phone had less than two dozen numbers listed, and if he was honest, several were only there out of habit. They were old faces from Salisbury, who he worked with that had retired. Gus wondered whether the numbers were even still valid. Four of the Detective Sergeants he had in his contacts list played golf. They probably moved to Spain without giving him their new number. Gus was unlikely to call them to find out.

If there was a burner phone, the few potential numbers were crucial to solving this case. Boddington was their best hope of finding that phone if it still existed.

Gus decided he would not make headway until they spoke to Patrick Boddington again in the morning. After that, it was time to head home. As he descended to the ground floor, he suddenly remembered that the Reverend was calling on him this evening. Gus wondered what news Clemency Bentham brought from Canada. The drive home to Urchfont dragged more than usual. The closer he got to his house, the more he realised that it couldn't be good news if Clemency wanted to tell him in person.

Once he was inside the bungalow, Gus faced another dilemma. When would Clemency arrive? Had she eaten? Gus called her.

Clemency answered on the second ring. The Reverend sounded out of breath,

"I'm on my way," she said, "I've stopped cycling, so I'm not breaking the law. I'll be with you in two minutes."

"Are you hungry?" asked Gus, "I've just got home from work, and I haven't eaten."

"I'm ravenous," said Clemency, "but I'm on a diet, and this cycling lark is to help get me fitter and lose weight. Unfortunately, if I tuck into something this evening, it will undo the good I've done since I started on Monday."

"I'll wait until we've had our face-to-face then," said Gus, "if it gets too late to cook, I'll order a takeaway. Don't worry. I won't flick through the various menu options while you're here. I hate watching people drool."

Gus watched from his lounge window after he'd ended the call. Two minutes later, on cue, a large lady on a bicycle sailed through the gateway. The warm June weather had encouraged the Reverend to wear a straw hat. It kept the sun off her rosy cheeks but looked an odd combination with her three-quarter-sleeved paisley blouse, dog collar, and black trousers.

Gus opened the door.

"Welcome to my humble abode," he said, "come indoors."

Clemency removed her straw hat and fanned herself.

"Gosh, I have never felt so unfit. I've always been a big girl, but since I moved to Urchfont, I seem to pile on the pounds. To grow my own fruit and vegetables was a wonderful idea at the time; now, I'm not so sure."

Gus smiled. They were in familiar territory.

"I know what you mean," he said. "When you grow them yourself, they taste better than the bought variety. Bert Penman advises us on what to grow and when and encourages us to plant far more than we would ever need. Then, when the crops are ready to harvest, we feel duty-bound to get them out of the ground and eat them while they're still at their best. I fell into that trap the first year I moved here. Tess had a fuller figure too, and she blamed me for the extra weight she acquired. I was too much of a gentleman to pass comment. I just altered my planting regime to include more salad items and fewer potatoes for next season."

"Perhaps you can dig out that planting regime for me," said Clemency, "it could prove beneficial."

"Come through to the lounge and make yourself comfortable," said Gus. "Can I get you a drink, Clemency? Non-alcoholic, if you prefer."

Clemency sank into one of Gus's comfortable chairs.

"I spy an excellent ten-year-old malt on the side table, Gus," said the Reverend, "I know I shouldn't, but the news I bring is awful."

"You said in your note that Bert was OK, but he had received dreadful news from Canada. What's happened?"

"There's been a terrible road accident. Bert's son, David, his wife, Lilian and their daughter, Virginia and her family were in a people carrier struck by a freight train on a grade-crossing. That's a level-crossing to you and me. All six passengers in the Peugeot died."

Gus stood up and walked across to his drinks cabinet. The Reverend was right; this was dreadful news. It was hard enough for him to take in, let alone Bert, what a thing to have to cope with at eighty-five. Nobody should have to bury a child, let alone an entire family wiped out in a split second.

"How old was David?" asked Gus as he handed Clemency a generous shot of McCallan's.

"He would have been sixty in August. Lilian was fifty-eight. Virginia was their youngest child, she was thirty-four, and her husband Logan Brown was thirty-eight. Their children, Nathan and Olivia, were thirteen and eleven. It's too horrible to contemplate."

"It's times like this that test your faith, I imagine," said Gus.

"No, my faith remains solid," said Clemency, "there's nothing I can do for those poor souls four thousand miles away except pray for them. My role is to help Bert get through this ordeal. He feels helpless because he knows he can't fly out for the funeral."

"Where did they live?" asked Gus.

"Saskatoon, in Saskatchewan," said Clemency, "the biggest city in the Province."

"It's easy to forget how vast Canada is," said Gus, "when did the accident happen? Do they know what caused it?"

"It happened on Monday evening, at around nine thirty-five," said Clemency. "The family was travelling home from a school function. The level-crossing gates lowered, preventing the Peugeot from crossing, and allowed an eastbound freight train to continue its route. After the train had passed, the gates rose, allowing David to cross. As he drove over the tracks, a second train, heading westward, struck the Peugeot. The people carrier split in two, and the rear half dragged a further eight hundred metres. The front half ended up on an embankment fifty metres from the level-crossing. Both front-seat passengers died instantly; the two adults and two children in the rear died of their injuries before they could reach the hospital."

"There have been so many tragic accidents on level-crossings over the years," said Gus, "surely, safety measures are in place to prevent this sort of tragedy?"

"Investigations are ongoing," said Clemency. "The level-crossing gates might have malfunctioned, but locals told the police that kids were always messing with the gates late in the evening. There were no eyewitnesses to support that theory. Dusk doesn't arrive for another thirty minutes. Few locals were outside their properties. It may have been a tragic accident."

"We must rally round," said Gus, "as we did when Frank North died. This village has an unbreakable community spirit. I know you'll find plenty of people offering to help Bert."

"That will not be the problem, and you know it, Gus," said Clemency. "It's getting the old buzzard to accept help in the first place."

"You've got him eating out of your hand, Clemency. I know I can rely on you. If there's anything I can do, just ask. My time is limited, but Bert is a diamond we need to treasure."

"I suppose I'd better get back on my trusty steed and cycle home," said Clemency. She plopped the straw hat on her head and levered her frame out of Gus's comfy chair.

"I should advise you against cycling home, madam. You could be liable to a fine of one thousand pounds if stopped, whether on the road or the pavement."

Clemency looked Gus straight in the eye.

"Is this how you get so many women to stay here, Gus? Ply them with drink and then persuade them that sleeping under your roof is better than a thousand pound fine? I'll be OK, and there's more of me to absorb that whisky than for you."

"I must correct you there, Clemency," said Gus. "First, I like to think it's my boyish charm that attracts them, but second, several variables can affect how quickly someone feels the effect of alcohol. How much body fat versus water their bodies comprise plays a major role. That's because alcohol is soluble in water but moves slowly through fat. When you drink alcohol, it distributes itself in tissues rich in water, like muscle, instead of those rich in fat. Pour alcohol into water, and it goes straight into solution. If you pour it into fat, the two will separate."

"You're no fun, Gus," said Clemency. "How many people have you lectured on science like this over the years?"

"Too many," said Gus, collecting his car keys. "Women reach a higher blood alcohol concentration than men of the same weight when they drink the same amount of alcohol. As a result, women's bodies tend to have more fat and less water than men's. Now, I'll run you home if you accept that you lost the argument. I've got bungee straps in the garden shed we can use to secure your bike to the boot of my car."

With Clemency seated in the passenger seat of the Focus, Gus secured her bone shaker safely to the back and made ready to drive her home. They were no sooner in the lane than Clemency had a thought.

"You had a decent measure of that McCallan's, too," she cried, "what if you get stopped?"

"We can always turn around, and I'll make up the spare bed," said Gus.

"Is there a lock on the door?"

"There is, so there's no danger of you getting into my room. I'll be perfectly safe."

"A sense of humour can be an attractive quality in a man," said Clemency, thumping Gus on the arm. "I'll revise my opinion; you don't seduce your women with a drink. You're just a lovely chap."

"Have you ever, you know?"

"I had a life before I got ordained, you know."

"Was there nobody serious?"

"Not really. I had several boyfriends as a teenager in Dorchester and up at Oxford University. After I completed my degree, I started work in the City as a data scientist. It was far less interesting than it sounds. All I ever seemed to do was work, eat, and sleep. Then, I woke up one morning and thought there had to be more to life."

"We've all thought that," said Gus, "and here we are at the vicarage,"

Gus got out and removed Clemency's bicycle from the back of the car. She stood on the pavement with her hands on the handlebars.

"I was twenty-eight when I saw the light," she said. "Since I donned the dog collar, I've loved every minute. My congregation make it so enjoyable. The only downside is that I haven't been on a date for five years. The collar scares them off, I suppose."

"What's next for Bert?" asked Gus, moving back to the driver's door. "When's the funeral?"

"Friday the fifteenth," said Clemency, "I'll stay with Bert for as long as I can that day. Irene North promised to help too. She asked me about Bert's eldest grandchild. Irene wondered what happened to him."

"I recall Bert telling me that David and his wife had two children. He said they were doing well in their careers. Did you ask Bert about the other child?"

"The son's name is Brett, and he's thirty-six. Bert told me Brett's a veterinary physician. He *was* married, but that ended three years ago. They didn't have children. It must be awful for Brett to be the only family member left. Bert's daughter, Margaret, who lives in New Zealand, will attend the funeral with her family. After that, Bert hopes they'll fit in a visit to the UK. You know Bert; he says he hopes they get here before he's called to meet his maker."

"So do I," said Gus, "we need Bert to hang around for much longer yet."

"I'd better let you get off home. The neighbours will talk. Thanks for the lift. Can I call you early next week to see when you're available to chat with Bert, to give him something else to occupy his mind?"

"Leave a message if I'm not there. It's never easy to make firm arrangements when a case throws up peculiar lines of enquiry."

"Goodnight, Gus. God bless."

The Reverend wheeled her bike up the path to the vicarage door, and Gus drove back to the bungalow. As he stood on the doorstep and lifted the key to the lock, he remembered he still hadn't eaten. Gus fished his phone out of his jacket pocket and ordered chicken curry with boiled rice from the nearest Chinese restaurant. If he weren't careful, he'd be putting on weight like the Reverend, but after learning Bert's terrible news, he needed a drink. It wasn't wise to do that on an empty stomach, regardless of how much water and body fat there was in his system. That was his excuse, and he was sticking to it.

Chapter Eight

Friday, 8 June 2018 - Devizes

GUS WAS awake at seven o'clock. He was too old for late-night takeaways and several glasses of Scotch. The brief walk to the shower was painful, and he stayed there far longer than usual to clear his head.

That was the actual problem, not the spicy food and hard liquor. Instead, it was thinking of Bert Penman's family and trying to make sense of Mark Malone's mystery activity. Even after he'd finished his second cup of black coffee before risking the drive to work, he still hadn't come up with any answers.

Gus parked the Focus in its usual spot and rode up in the lift to the CRT office. He was the first to arrive. The clock on the wall said it was twenty minutes to nine. The cast of characters for the night Mark Malone died should be his priority.

Gus cleared a whiteboard and added the names he could confirm had contacted Mark, either by text or phone.

Jenny Malone, Julian Drummond, Patrick Boddington.

Mark had contact with Damian Hartley-Cole besides the other three.

Gus couldn't put names on the four men who attended the sex party. Did it matter? He didn't believe they had anything to do with Mark's death.

So, who else might they need to identify? The driver of the black SUV. Was he alone, or did that car carry several passengers?

What about the other BMW? A similar problem.

The case was a nightmare. It was worse than tackling a jigsaw with a missing piece. Gus didn't even know how many they needed.

Luke Sherman was first out of the lift at five minutes to nine. He stopped at the board before going to his desk.

"It's sparse, isn't it, guv?" he said, "what about the weapon?"

"We know the make and model," said Gus, "but although I don't have names for several people on that board, I don't see anyone that might have owned it."

"I was thinking of what Lydia suggested," said Luke, "spreading the net wider. She traced the names of gang members who might have attacked Mark Allison. As she pointed out, one of those men could have inherited the weapon used to kill Mark Malone. What if they were in the black SUV?"

"I'll take Lydia with me this morning," said Gus, "when she gets here. That list of names should be in her Freeman Files section. Check with her before we leave. While we're in Bath, you can build backgrounds for those gang members. First, we need to discover where they've been since Mark Allison died and what they've been doing. Next, contact Damian Hartley-Cole and ask him for the exact date of the party near Salisbury, where the SUV first surfaced. Damian will avoid giving any details of the precise location, but the date is important. After that, we can fill in a few of the blanks ourselves. Then, make sure the same criminals, if you've got any names left, might have been in Newbury the night Mark Malone died. I do not doubt that the list will get smaller with every step you follow. If a name Lydia identified could be present on every occasion, we need to get them picked up and interviewed."

Lydia arrived just as the clock clicked around to nine o'clock.

"The traffic's terrible, guv," she said, "are we using my Mini again today?"

Gus smiled.

"I can always rely on you, Lydia," he said, "no, we'll take my car today. Chat with Luke while I grab my things, and then we'll battle through the traffic to Bath. I can't wait to meet this Patrick Boddington character."

Luke Sherman realised Lydia was non-plussed. She was wondering what Gus meant by being able to rely on her. Lydia wouldn't let him down and not turn up for work without a phone call. Luke had appreciated what their boss meant.

Patrick Boddington dressed in a style one could describe as theatrical and ostentatious. Yet, in the company that he kept, Patrick never got outshone. There was only space in his world for one peacock.

When Lydia arrived at the art gallery in an hour, poor Patrick faced a challenge like never before.

Lydia's coppery red hair seemed to have gained more corkscrews overnight. Her top was pure Jackson Pollock, and the short black leather skirt only emphasised what a magnificent pair of legs she had. Luke couldn't imagine how she walked anywhere in those four-inch high heels.

Neil Davis mentioned that Gus told Lydia to tone things down when they interviewed the public. On this occasion, Gus realised that Lydia had pitched the message correctly. Gus wanted Boddington on the back foot from the second they walked through the door. Lydia wouldn't make Boddington take a step back. The poor chap would be reeling.

"Can you give me the names of the gang members you identified, please, Lydia," Luke asked. "The ones which might have killed Mark Allison."

"Is Gus OK?" asked Lydia, opening the relevant file. "Here you are."

"Gus's fine," said Luke, "thanks, enjoy your morning in Bath."

Lydia trotted to the lift, where Gus stood waiting.

"Ready?" Gus asked.

"What time did Luke tell Mr Boddington to be ready for us, guv?"

"Ten o'clock, why?

"If you're driving, we'd better get moving."

Friday, 8 June 2018 - Portishead

DOMINIC CULVERHOUSE DROVE into the Avon and Somerset Police HQ in Valley Road, Portishead. He parked in his usual spot and walked towards the main building. Once inside, he asked at Reception for the room where the preliminary meeting would take place. Dominic had arrived with time to spare. He understood what awaited him.

A panel with an Independent Legally Qualified Chair would conduct any future hearing. The other panel members would be an officer of at least the rank of Superintendent and independent layperson selected from an approved list held by the office of the Police and Crime Commissioner. The panel heard the facts of the case. Witnesses assisted if required, and the panel decided whether the accused had committed gross misconduct.

Dominic hoped today's meeting prevented any of that from happening. He prepared as well for this as he had for any promotion board. As the subject of allegations, he could be accompanied or represented by a police friend in the proceedings.

The wily Assistant Chief Constable knew it was essential to pick his friend with care. When you set your sights on the top of the mountain, you inevitably clamber over others less able and committed than yourself. So, Culverhouse had no regrets about making dozens of enemies as he rose through the ranks.

His fellow travellers from the Masons were staunch supporters, and he knew things about several of them they wished to protect. Of course, none of them would ever go as far as him to preserve their status, but in his hour of need, Dominic believed he had selected just the right person to sit beside him in this preliminary meeting.

Culverhouse felt the first seeds of doubt as he paced the floor outside the meeting room with the clock ticking closer to the appointed start time. Was Guy Templeman going to fail him? Had the implied threat of disclosure of the West Mercia Chief Constable's extra-marital affair been a mistake? Was Guy prepared to walk away from his thirty-year marriage to live with the thirty-six-year-old head-teacher from his son's academy?

Culverhouse needn't have worried.

"Sorry to cut it fine, Dominic," said Guy as he hurried along the corridor to greet him. The handshake was firm and familiar. All doubts soon got dispelled. The two senior officers strode towards the door of the meeting room.

The IOPC Operations Team Leader brought the meeting to order on the dot of ten o'clock. Two Lead Investigators, Aysha Prasanna and Steve Nobbs, made up the IOPC team.

Madeleine Lefevre asked if the officer concerned received written notification of the details of the investigation. Dominic Culverhouse nodded his agreement. She then asked if they had explained his rights to him. The right to seek advice from his staff association. The right to have a police friend to accompany and represent him. The right to legal representation. Madeleine stressed that this meeting determined whether there was a case to answer. If so, Dominic Culverhouse would hear within five days and be required to return to Valley Road for a full hearing.

Dominic Culverhouse said he understood and waived his rights for legal representation and advice from his staff association. He introduced his police friend, the Chief Constable for West Mercia, Guy Templeman.

The IOPC Team Leader set out the meeting procedure, and Guy Templeman confirmed that the process was in line with regulations. The meeting was ready to begin.

"This investigation centres around the events of the twenty-second and twenty-third of September 2012," began Madeleine Lefevre. "Jason Whitworth, a twenty-two-year-old hotel worker from Basingstoke, was cycling home in driving rain on the B3400 Andover Road. A vehicle that failed to stop struck him, and a passing motorist found Jason's bicycle and body in a ditch by the side of the road the following morning. Can you tell us where you were on the dates in question?"

"I was attending the tenth annual class reunion for course attendees from Bramshill Police College," replied Culverhouse. "We stayed in Oakley or Basingstoke and met for a celebratory meal at Oakley Hall. There were sixteen senior officers in total."

"How did you arrive at Oakley Hall?"

"I drove from my home near Hereford on Saturday afternoon and booked into the Red Lion hotel for one night."

"Do you recall the car you drove?"

"A Porsche Boxster. Look, I had no idea what this hit-and-run had to do with me when I got contacted. I'm beginning to see how the misunderstanding occurred."

"How did you get to Oakley Hall on Saturday evening?"

"I drove, of course, and Sandra Plunkett hitched a lift because she was staying at the same hotel. It made sense, as we'd met on the course in 2002. It was long ago, but Sandra travelled by train in 2012. On previous reunions, she'd driven from wherever she was working. Look, I appreciate you want to stick to your procedure, but there's a simple, if unfortunate, answer to this mess. Sandra offered to drive back to Basingstoke so that I could have a drink. I'm sure you've checked with other people who attended. Guy Templeman was there and provided a statement before this meeting. Sandra had two or three drinks. Whether she was fit to drive when we left Oakley Hall, I was in no fit state to tell you. I accept my conduct was less than it should have been. As police officers, we're supposed to act with honesty and integrity at all times, both on and off duty. Sandra must have helped me to the car and strapped me in. I passed out. I remember nothing of the journey back to the Red Lion. I realised I couldn't drive to Hereford on Sunday morning until after lunch. I stayed in my room for as long as possible and then mooched around the hotel drinking black coffee. Sandra left for the train station before I was well enough to get out of bed. I didn't get the chance to thank her for looking after me. How would I know anything untoward had happened? I still didn't think along the lines of a hit-and-run even when I ventured into the car park. The front nearside wing of my Boxster was damaged. I cursed Sandra, thinking she'd hit the industrial-sized waste bin when she parked. I couldn't believe she hadn't waited to tell me. The car was only two years old. Perhaps Sandra had more to drink than I thought. I called her on Monday morning, but she said she hadn't noticed, and there was no cause for her to look at my car the next morning. She was intent on packing her bags and not missing the Birmingham train."

"Were you surprised that your Porsche Boxster was still on the road?"

"Why?" asked Culverhouse. "The damage wasn't severe. I drove the car to Hereford later in the day. I just felt I had to get rid of it."

"Why?" asked Madeleine Lefevre.

"I loved that car," said Culverhouse, "but it would always bear the scars of that incident in the car park. Well, that's how I viewed it. I did not understand what caused the damage until I received notification of this investigation. With hindsight, I can see what must have happened. Sandra Plunkett hit the cyclist while driving an unfamiliar car in driving rain. You can't ask now whether she knew she had hit him or whether she was unfit to drive. Sandra parked my car by the waste bins to hide or disguise the damage and walked upstairs to bed. How I got to my room, I don't recall. I was fully clothed when I awoke. I've been in contact with the other fourteen officers over the past six years. There was never a suspicion that a dreadful accident occurred while we celebrated our tenth reunion. How Sandra lived with herself, I've no idea. Well, now the truth was coming out. She couldn't live with herself. She took her own life and that of her partner, an innocent in this. You think you know someone…."

"We have found no one to support your story that Sandra Plunkett drove the car that night, nor that she was drunk. So how do you explain that?"

"May I say something?" asked Guy Templeman.

"We have your statement, Chief Constable. Do you wish to add something to that?"

"It's time to come clean, just like Dominic," he said, "a good number of us were very drunk that night. I stayed the night at Oakley Hall, and the same as Dominic, I'm not sure how I reached my room. I'm not surprised anybody confirmed who drove the Porsche on the return journey. Only a handful of people were in the car park outside the Hall. As for determining whether poor Sandra was fit to drive, there was only one sober man among us. At the time, he was a Chief Superintendent in the Surrey force based in Guildford. Maurice Kennedy died of pancreatic cancer in 2016. Even if he was still alive, there's no guarantee he hadn't driven off with his three passengers before Sandra got Dominic to the car. None of those who spent the night at Oakley knew what happened after the reunion party ended."

Madeleine Lefevre sat back in her chair. She glanced left and right. Where did they go next? Her two lead investigators, Aysha Prasanna and Steve Nobbs sat stony-faced. Madeleine wasn't getting much help from their direction.

When the IOPC first received the files outlining offences committed by the officers concerned, things looked promising. Wiltshire Police had done an excellent job. Who could have foreseen that so many people involved in the case would die before proceedings got underway?

According to Guy Templeman, Maurice Kennedy, the only sober man among the revellers, died two years ago. Sandra Plunkett, accused of the crime in 2012, committed suicide days ago. So it was very convenient for the man seated opposite. Madeleine studied the smug bastard. She had never met Dominic Culverhouse, but as soon as he walked into the room this morning, she instantly disliked him.

Culverhouse considered the meeting was beneath him, and he wanted everyone on her side of the table to know it. If only there were more than a slap on the wrist for conduct unbecoming to throw at the man.

By their admission, Culverhouse and Templeman were at Oakley, where members of the public and staff watched while more than a dozen officers got so drunk they could barely stand. Madeleine imagined her superiors wanting to sweep the affair under the carpet. Why bother with a minor misdemeanour from six years earlier? The big prize was off the table. The IOPC didn't want to leave themselves open to criticism that they only pursued soft targets.

"Can we wrap up this charade now?" asked Culverhouse. "I think you have wasted enough of our time. I've explained what must have happened. It's the only logical explanation."

Madeleine played her last card.

"When did you first meet Ricky Gardiner?"

"I'm not sure I've heard the name," replied Culverhouse, "who is he; what does he do?"

"He worked for the Metropolitan Police for thirty years, much of that time he spent undercover, mixing with the worst kind of criminal. He was successful at what he did, but his handlers lost touch with him so often that they could never decide whether he was working for them or against them. So when he left the Met, he offered his services as a fixer. Someone who got the job done, no questions asked, for a fee. So Gardiner worked on both sides of the law, something it's suspected he had done for many years."

"He sounds a fascinating character," said Culverhouse, "but not in tune with modern policing. So how is he relevant to this conversation?"

"Ricky Gardiner died in a fire in London earlier this week," said Madeleine. "Can you tell me where you were on Tuesday between six and midnight?"

"I finished work at six. Afterwards, I visited a restaurant, ate a meal, drank in two pubs on the way back to my hotel, and then spent the rest of the evening reading. I was in bed by around ten-thirty."

"Where was this?" asked Aysha Prasanna.

"Greenwich," said Culverhouse.

"You've chosen to work during your suspension rather than take gardening leave, is that correct?" asked Aysha.

"That's correct."

"Can you give us the names of the places you visited during the evening and the name of the hotel where you stayed?" asked Steve Nobbs.

"I could take you there, but I'm unfamiliar with the district. However, I can tell you the hotel's name before I leave."

"How did you pay for your meal and drinks?" asked Steve.

"Cash. Look, where is this going? Are you on another

fishing expedition? I said I hadn't met this Gardiner fellow. Do you have any proof we ever met? How does he connect to the Oakley business? Sandra Plunkett might have known him. I'll be on my way unless you have something concrete to put before me. Then, your superiors will hear from me. This pantomime has gone on long enough."

Madeleine Lefevre sensed a pinch of panic in Dominic Culverhouse's latest outburst.

If only they had more concrete evidence.

"I can't understand why you're in such a rush to leave," she said. "Your suspension will stay in place until the IOPC is satisfied with your answers. You haven't convinced me you were blameless in matters that occurred at Oakley. However, a series of unfortunate events may have provided you with an unshakeable alibi for now. Within hours of receiving notice of suspension, you contacted a close friend and transferred to Greenwich. I'm not too fond of coincidences, and Ricky Gardiner died the day after you moved there. That worries me. I found it significant that you chose to work in the neighbouring borough to where Gardiner slept on Tuesday the fifth of June."

"I'd never heard of Gardiner before you mentioned him," said Culverhouse, "how could I know where he might live?"

"As a senior police officer, you have access to many methods of gaining information. That wasn't where he lived. It was merely a flat at which he arranged the option to stay. Gardiner was a complicated character. Some might say devious. It would take someone with a similar skill set to find him."

"I've explained that I played no part in the hit-and-run scandal," said Culverhouse. "Now you're making wild assumptions just because I stayed in London at the same time as someone I'd never met. Do you see how ludicrous that sounds? Guy, you can appreciate now why I said former colleagues with Wiltshire Police are hellbent on revenge. The truth they can't accept is that I progressed, and they didn't. It's so petty; it's laughable."

"When you're ready," said Madeleine, "we'll continue. We asked Greenwich to supply CCTV images from Tuesday evening, tracking your movements from when you left Royal Hill, Greenwich, until you arrived at Novotel on Greenwich High Road. Do you wish to reconsider what you've told us?"

Dominic Culverhouse sat further back in his seat. Madeleine opened a folder containing hard copies of CCTV images.

"You left the office Greenwich allocated you at one minute past six. This image shows you exiting the building wearing the uniform of an ACC with Avon and Somerset Police. Any comment?"

"No, why should there be? I told you I left at six," replied Culverhouse.

"The Guildford Arms is five minute's walk from the police station. Here you are entering the gastropub at ten past seven. You are now wearing a black top and dark slacks. Did you pop into a phone box en route? How do you explain the change in clothing?"

"I returned to the hotel to change. I couldn't go out for the evening wearing my uniform."

"Would you say dark clothing, such as we can see in the image from the gastropub, is typical of what you might wear on a warm summer evening?"

"I had to leave Hereford in a rush," said Culverhouse, "I didn't give my wardrobe much thought. I just grabbed a few spare shirts, a pair of trousers, and clean underwear."

"This image shows you leaving the Guildford Arms alone ninety minutes later."

"Do you plan to take me on a whistle-stop tour of Greenwich pubs? I can't see the purpose of this line of questioning. I'm a single man on a night out. So what?"

"What tasks were you given at Royal Hill to occupy your days?" asked Steve Nobbs. "I imagine if you get parachuted into a station at a minute's notice, it must limit your contribution. Also, you don't know the people you're working with and are unfamiliar with the locality or caseload they're handling."

"An Assistant Chief Constable is well-equipped to adapt," said Guy Templeman. "Dominic's wealth of experience in policing would be a welcome addition to any force. His rank equates to a Commander in the Metropolitan Police. I wouldn't expect Greenwich to have had him performing basic office duties."

"So, you attended strategy meetings related to your responsibilities at Portishead. You hold the portfolio for crime in the Avon and Somerset area. Is that correct?"

"That's correct."

"We'll check that workload with your superiors at Royal Hill. You told us earlier that after your meal, you visited several pubs and returned to your hotel by ten o'clock," said Madeleine Lefevre. "There were discrepancies in your account of the first part of the evening. Would you like to amend anything you mentioned about your whereabouts between twenty minutes to nine and ten o'clock?"

"No," said Culverhouse, "but I don't remember which pubs I visited. There are quite a few, and wherever I went wasn't more than a mile from the hotel. I suppose you will show me in the Dog and Duck with a pint in my hand? Is this how this goes?"

"Well, here's the thing," said Madeleine. "As a policeman who is well-equipped to handle any eventuality, you know, despite over six hundred thousand cameras in the London area, black spots can still exist. The next sighting of you shows you in the foyer of Novotel at nine forty-eight. Do you notice anything in this piece of video we recovered?"

"I'm still wearing the same clothing I wore in the Guild-ford Arms. I'm steady on my feet. So, it confirms that I didn't visit more than two pubs. So, what am I supposed to be looking for?"

"We can see three other guests in the foyer. They pass through without looking directly towards the camera. It would be difficult if we wished to identify them using this camera position. The manager stressed this camera was essential to protect the reception staff. You linger in the vicinity without approaching the reception desk, and your face is in full view on three occasions. Almost as if you wanted proof, you were in the hotel by ten o'clock as you claimed."

"I suppose you will tell me I don't have an alibi for the intervening sixty-eight minutes. Forgive me, but I've no clue where or when this man Gardiner died. This is ridiculous. I told you I could take you to the pubs where I drank. Someone should remember serving me."

"Can you confirm you never left the borough of Green-wich between leaving the Guildford Arms and reaching your hotel?" asked Madeleine.

"As I keep telling you, I'm unfamiliar with the district. Where did one borough end and another start? I walked between one watering hole and another, and it took only ten minutes to get back to my hotel when I decided it was time to get to bed."

"Let's leave that unexplained sixty-eight minutes for now," said Madeleine, "where did you park your car during your stay?"

"In the Novotel car park. I had the offer of a parking space at Royal Hill, but I left my car at the hotel and walked to work each day. It's only a five minute walk."

"Does the hotel have CCTV coverage of the car park?"

"I should sincerely hope so," said Culverhouse.

"We requested the records from six pm Tuesday to six am Wednesday. We noted several bursts of activity, with guests arriving and leaving the car park in the first few hours. Then, at five minutes past ten, we have a figure slipping out of the car park entrance on foot, in dark clothing."

"That could be anybody," said Guy Templeman. "the hotel has over one hundred and fifty guest rooms, conference facilities and many staff members. That person is wearing a dark-coloured hooded jacket and carrying a backpack. The face is obscured. I think it is impossible to identify them."

"I was in my room reading," said Culverhouse.

"Might I suggest we take a break?" asked Guy Templeman. "Dominic has answered your questions relating to the Oakley affair, which was the main substance of the complaint against him. There was no mention of another investigation into the death of the mystery man, Ricky Gardiner. I'm at a loss to understand the proof of any connection between Dominic and Gardiner. As Dominic suggested, you're joining the dots between two sets of unrelated events and attempting to show what? That Dominic had a reason to kill Gardiner? The man died in a fire. Where was this, and at what time? Just because Dominic was five miles up the road doesn't mean he's culpable. How many crimes got reported on Tuesday evening within a five-mile radius of where Dominic stayed? Twenty? Fifty? Why not charge him with all of them? I think checking every pub between the Guildford Arms and the hotel is simpler. That removes any possibility of Dominic being anywhere other than Greenwich. If you can offer definitive proof of a connection between Gardiner and Dominic, then produce it when we reconvene. If not, then I support Dominic's desire to walk out. This witch hunt should have concluded once he'd explained the Oakley matter."

Madeleine Lefevre accepted she was getting nowhere. If only they had found that elusive connection or confirmed the money trail—just something to wipe the smile off Culverhouse's face.

"I agree," she said, "we need a break."

Chapter Nine

Friday, 8 June 2018 - Bath

"HEAD FOR MANVERS STREET CAR PARK," said Lydia, "that's closest to the Abbey, isn't it?"

"It's never a hardship walking through Bath," said Gus, "it's a beautiful city."

"Whenever I visit, it's raining when I arrive, or it starts just as I'm heading home."

"Not today," said Gus, "there's hardly a cloud in the sky. Right, do you have any change? I appear to have come out without my wallet."

"How many hours will we need?" asked Lydia, searching through her purse.

"Oh, only two," said Gus, "I don't intend to suffer another life story."

"Touché," said Lydia, "it won't happen again, guv."

Gus and Lydia strode towards North Parade.

"Which is the quickest route from here?" asked Gus.

Lydia led him through a maze of side streets and alleyways until they emerged in the Abbey Courtyard. The wide, open space was full of people, mostly tourists.

"Where's Boddington's gallery?" asked Lydia.

"Dead ahead," said Gus, "between the café and the bookshop. Try not to knock over any pedestrians or street performers on the way."

Gus heard the Abbey clock in the Tower to his right gather itself for a peal of bells. Ten o'clock. Despite Lydia's concerns over his driving, they'd made it on time.

Gus and Lydia reached the safety of the covered entrance to the gallery. The door was set back six feet from the paved courtyard. Behind the glass windows surrounding them, they could see a selection of oil paintings featuring city views. There were plenty from which to choose.

"You go first, Lydia," said Gus. "make the introductions. I want a few seconds to get the measure of the man."

"You want me to take the lead?" asked Lydia. "I wish I'd worn something newer rather than thrown on this old thing. What are you like?"

Gus shook his head. You can't win them all.

Lydia pushed open the door. Gus heard a delicate tinkle above him and looked back at the bell on the back of the door. He'd not seen that design for half a century.

Gus remembered visiting a sweet shop in Salisbury with his mother at five years old. He didn't imagine Patrick Boddington stocked sherbet dabs or gobstoppers, and there wasn't an old master among his paintings either. In the shadow of the Abbey, Patrick Boddington surrendered pretensions to fine art years ago. Instead, he chased the tourist trade these days.

Gus wondered whether tourists wanted a large oil painting of the Royal Crescent or the Roman Baths to add to hand luggage on their return journey. But of course, you can capture everything of historical importance on a phone's camera these days.

Most people preferred to include themselves in such well-known images with a selfie, in case their friends hadn't realised where they'd gone on holiday.

Gus studied a picture of Jane Austen's house and thought it looked better without two grinning Japanese tourists extending their selfie sticks. Although at three hundred and fifty pounds, that painting would never find itself on a wall in his Urchfont bungalow.

Patrick Boddington appeared from behind a pair of heavy drapes separating his office from the gallery.

Lydia expected something theatrical. Appearing on stage like a latter-day Sir John Gielgud was more than she imagined.

"We're quiet this morning," he said, "I'll turn the sign around to deter any customers. They browse the books next door, then have a look at everything I have to offer. The café is so popular that they have to queue for a table. As soon as someone's bum lifts off a seat next door, they're out of here. Well, you can't *both* be from the constabulary. You two make as unlikely a pair as Sonny and Cher."

"My name is Ms Barre. I work in the Crime Review Team from Wiltshire Police. My boss, Mr Freeman, wants to follow up on the questions you answered yesterday."

Gus studied Boddington while Lydia made the introductions. The gallery owner stood five feet, six inches tall and weighed nine stones wringing wet. Patrick's Sixties style suit was in maroon velvet, and his shirt was navy blue, as was the keffiyeh draped around his shoulders. He had no bouffant hairstyle or comb-over. Instead, Patrick opted for the polished, shaved head look. His half-moon spectacles with navy blue frames completed the ensemble.

Luke Sherman said Boddington reminded him of Quentin Crisp. Gus had done his homework last night as he devoured his chicken curry. One of Crisp's quotes floated into his head: - *Exhibitionism is like a drug. Be yourself no matter what they say.*

As he looked at Patrick and Lydia, it was hard to find fault with that observation.

"I thought I'd satisfied your colleague," said Patrick, "what do you need now?"

"It's quite straightforward," said Gus, "we know from Mark Malone's phone records that you spoke to one another twice on the night he died."

"Poor Mark. I think of him often," said Patrick.

"You called him at a quarter to twelve," said Lydia, "and spoke for two minutes."

"Did I? Well, if you say I did, then I suppose I must have. It's so long ago."

"I'll remind you for the last time that we're investigating a murder enquiry, Mr Boddington," said Gus. "I'm not here for the fun of it. You and Mark had been lovers. When we spoke to Jenny Malone, she told us you and Mark remained firm friends. You saw one another regularly and often dined together."

"That's true. We never fell out. The physical side of our relationship died."

"Right, back to the night in question. Did you know where Mark went that night? Had he told you he was partying in Newbury? Was there a prior arrangement for you to call?"

"I knew where Mark was going," said Patrick, playing with the tassels on his keffiyeh. "He asked me to call him. Mark wanted an excuse to get away from the party. My call should have been earlier, but I was with someone. When I remembered to call, he was already on his way home to Bath. Mark was short with me."

"Why did he call back after midnight?" asked Lydia, "it must have been important. You spoke for seven minutes."

"Mark thought someone followed him," said Patrick, "I urged him to phone the police, but Mark said he couldn't."

"Did he say where he was?" asked Gus.

"Mark stopped at a garage because there were bright lights and other people around. He felt safer. Mark was talking to me, and I suddenly heard a noise. Mark said a man was banging on the window and shouting at him."

"Did he recognise the man?" asked Gus.

"I don't know," said Patrick.

"Why would someone follow him?" asked Lydia.

"It had something to do with the dogs."

"Did Mark get involved in something criminal?" asked Gus.

"He wouldn't have confided in me if he did," said Patrick.

"You knew one another for a long time," said Gus, "what did you think when Mark started driving around in a top-of-the-range BMW?"

"I loved cruising around Bath in that car with Mark. It felt so decadent. You could do all sorts of things behind those tinted windows. How on earth he afforded it, I don't know."

"Mark didn't ask you for money?" asked Gus.

"Heaven's, no, I've hardly got two pennies to rub together these days. The gallery barely gives me enough to scrape by. My companions pay for any extravagances."

"What happened to Mark's apartment in Marlborough Lane?" asked Lydia.

"Mark rented it, my dear; he didn't own it. The landlady changed the locks, refreshed the paintwork, and moved in a young couple two months after Mark died. The police kept going backwards and forwards to no avail before that."

"I suppose you threw your key away?" asked Gus.

"Well, I didn't have any further use for it, did I?" said Patrick.

"The conversation you described at the garage didn't occupy the whole seven minutes," said Gus. "So, what else did you discuss?"

"Whatever prompted the banging on the window died down," said Patrick, "and Mark drove away from the garage forecourt. He told me the car that scared him had reappeared two hundred yards behind. He'd been waiting further up the road."

"What did you do?" asked Gus.

"I begged him to call the police. Or to let me call them."

"Did he tell you what car it was?" asked Lydia.

"Mark said it was a black SUV," said Patrick.

"So, Mark was being followed to Devizes by a black SUV, and he felt in danger. Was that the end of the conversation?"

Patrick looked at the wall behind Gus's head. He avoided eye contact.

"Remember what I said earlier," said Gus.

"Mark asked me to remove something from the flat if something happened to him."

"How did you know where to look if Mark never confided in you about his dodgy dealings?"

"I didn't know a thing, I swear," said Patrick, "Mark had a mobile phone he didn't want the police to discover. So I promised him I'd find it."

"When did you learn of Mark's death?" asked Lydia.

"Jenny called me after she returned from the hospital.

She was distraught, but I was still the first person she contacted, for which I was grateful. I walked to the flat within minutes of her call. The police didn't arrive with their vans and blue-and-white tape until lunchtime; I watched them from across the road. Then, after shutting the flat door for the last time, I'd popped in to visit an old friend. He made us several Irish coffees to see me through the worst."

"Was there anything other than the mobile phone worth having?" asked Gus.

"What sort of person do you think I am?" asked Patrick.

"When did the police come to interview you?" asked Lydia.

"They didn't. Someone from Manvers Street phoned me two days after the murder. I went to the police station to make a statement. I told them I had spoken to Mark and that someone had shouted at him when he stopped at the garage. They wanted to know about our relationship, not that it was any of their business. I had witnesses to say I never left Bath that night and that we were still friends. The police were happy enough with that. The last time anyone spoke with me, they intimated that road rage was the probable cause for Mark getting shot. I'm eternally glad I never learned to drive."

"You omitted to mention the black SUV and the mobile phone to the police," said Gus, "why was that?"

"I promised Mark I wouldn't let the police get hold of the phone. I didn't understand why it was significant, but I didn't want his reputation blackened when he couldn't defend himself. As for the SUV, I thought the police knew about it. They had CCTV coverage of the garage and knew the man shouting at Mark drove another BMW. The police officer at Manvers Street mentioned it."

"Where's that phone now?" asked Gus.

"In landfill somewhere," said Patrick. "it was no use to me. Why would I need another phone? I got rid of it at the earliest opportunity."

"Did you open it?" asked Lydia, "was it password protected?"

Patrick looked at Gus.

"Mark must have got mixed up in something awful," he said, "or you wouldn't be so interested in that phone three years after he died. So what was he doing?"

"If only we knew," said Gus, "you thought the dogs were a possibility. We've talked to others who breed and show dogs, but there doesn't appear to be a fortune to gain from breeding. Dogs of popular breeds get smuggled into the UK, and that trade must be profitable because there's enough money in the enterprise for organised crime gangs to get involved. Perhaps Mark earned money for that BMW by accepting smuggled dogs to sell in his pet shop. That wouldn't generate large sums of money because you can be sure the gang took the lion's share of any profit. If a gang member followed Mark in that black SUV, it suggests Mark owed someone money. We need to find that man and uncover the truth."

"Poor Mark," said Patrick. "Now, what can I tell you about that phone? Well, it wasn't a smartphone. It didn't have any fancy apps that I could see; and only two names were in his contact list. The phone *was* password-protected, but I'd known Mark for too long. It was Labia Syphre. He'd kept threatening to become a drag queen. That was to be his stage name. Mark thought it hilarious."

"Do you remember either of the contact names?" asked Lydia.

"I remember both. Emir Pompey and Mehmet Barking," replied Patrick, "they're not details you forget. One of them killed Mark."

"Were they Turkish?" asked Gus.

"Their names are foreign, but I never met them. So I expect Mark did what he usually did," said Patrick, "and added where they came from or what they did for a living to their first name. It helped him remember who they were and where he'd met them. He had a long list of names to remember."

"We know that from the mobile phone in his car the night he died," said Lydia. She wondered whether Patrick knew how Mark remembered his best friend.

"Can you remember any details of the call history?" asked Gus.

"I don't know if it's significant," said Patrick, "but Mark only ever spoke to them. There were no text messages back and forth."

"That was so no record of their conversations existed to be used against them if their phones ever got lost or stolen," said Lydia.

Gus nodded.

"I think we can discount them being legitimate dog owners or breeders. What about the frequency of calls? Can you recall something that might help?"

"You'll think I was nosy, but I skipped through to see how long they had been in touch with Mark. The call log dates back to February 2014, when Emir made the first contact. Mehmet didn't start calling Mark until August. The calls came a month to six weeks apart. On Friday, before Mark died, there were three conversations. On Saturday afternoon, there was just one. Mark left the phone in the flat when he drove to Newbury, and a missed call registered on the phone came from Emir at around half-past seven."

"The gang were desperate to get hold of Mark," said Lydia.

"He must have told them on Friday where he was going," said Gus, "perhaps Emir called to check Mark had left home. So we've got two first names to match with gang members connected to the murder weapon."

"Luke should have reduced the size of our list of names by the time we get back to the office," said Lydia, "is there anything else, guv?"

"Nothing, unless Mr Boddington can remember what he removed from Mark's flat on Sunday morning."

"You won't leave it alone, will you? A few engraved trinkets I'd bought for Mark," sighed Patrick, "and a Lalique bowl. I told Jenny about that. She was happy for me to have it."

"You appear to have potential customers outside, Mr Boddington," said Gus, "we'll let you re-open your shop."

"Gallery, Mr Freeman, if you please, a shop sounds common, and these are original oil paintings, you know. They might not be by Turner or Rembrandt, but there's no a print among them."

Patrick Boddington turned the 'Closed' sign on the glass door to 'Open', and Gus savoured the bell's chime for the second time as he and Lydia strode through the open door onto the Abbey courtyard. They had two names. Would these two Turks be the key to solving this case?

Friday, 8 June 2018 - Portishead

CHIEF CONSTABLE GUY Templeman was a busy man. He wanted to get out of this building and drive back to West

Mercia HQ at Worcester. Guy's force area covered Hereford, where Dominic Culverhouse lived. Something he would happily alter if he could.

The longer that morning meeting went on, the less he trusted the man he thought was a friend. Even though Lefevre and her team couldn't deliver a knockout punch, Guy couldn't shake the feeling that Dominic lied on more than one occasion.

Madeleine Lefevre had wanted this break as much as he had.

While Dominic spent the last two hours drinking coffee and complaining he was the victim of character assassination designed to prevent him from becoming a Chief Constable, Guy wondered whether he'd backed the wrong horse.

"How much longer do I have to hang around here?" asked Dominic.

Guy watched him pacing. Culverhouse didn't fill him with any confidence; he looked nervous and agitated. At the start of the day, Guy thought it only natural to have a few nerves, but now he thought it suspicious.

"You'll wear the carpet out if you don't sit and relax," said Guy, "we reconvene at two o'clock. Is there anything you need to tell me before we go back inside?"

"Don't you start," shouted Culverhouse, "they're fishing. The Oakley matter is dead in the water. It's all very well saying because Plunkett and Kennedy are dead; it provides me with an alibi. You were there that weekend, as were a dozen others. Have they interrogated them? Yes, they have. Has one person pointed the finger at me to say I drove my car that night? No, they haven't, and nobody could."

"Calm down, Dominic," said Guy Templeman.

Even though he had his doubts, Guy realised that his

integrity would be questioned by accepting the role of 'police friend' at this preliminary meeting. If things went pear-shaped for Culverhouse, Guy could suffer from the fallout. He had travelled too far in his career to see that happen.

Steve Nobbs stuck his head around the door of the waiting room.

"Five minutes, gentlemen. We're ready for you."

"Thank goodness," said Culverhouse, "let's wrap up this nonsense and get home."

Guy Templeman and Dominic Culverhouse walked along the corridor to the meeting room. Madeleine Lefevre poured herself a glass of water from a carafe on the table. She looked up as the two officers entered.

Guy Templeman thought Lefevre looked more confident than when they last saw her. What had she learned in the interim?

"I hope you benefited from the break as much as we did," said Madeleine, "what is it they say? Everything comes to she who waits. We received information from the detectives investigating the deaths of Sandra Plunkett and Naomi Hall."

"I suppose you're trying to pin that on me, too," said Culverhouse.

"There's no question they committed suicide," said Aysha Prasanna. "What drove them to it is another matter."

"Among the items recovered from the home shared by the two women were three mobile phones," said Madeleine. "They found proof of purchase and original packaging for two phones that showed they belonged to Sandra and Naomi. The third phone appeared to be the odd one out. There was no record of it on any of their insurance documents. Nothing in either of their bank statements suggested they bought it. Forensics dusted the phone for prints, and Sandra was the only person to handle it. Why did she need it? Was it issued to her by Wiltshire Police? The Staffordshire detectives checked, and Wiltshire confirmed it was not. What did the phone contain? The contact list held two numbers. Sadly, we can't ask Sandra why she named them A and B. Contact A's phone appeared out of service. Who knows, perhaps it got destroyed? Contact B's phone was still in service, and the phone rang and rang without anyone answering. In the past two hours, GPS tracking located that phone. It's somewhere in Croydon."

"What's the point of this analysis of the Staffordshire Police investigation?" asked Guy Templeman. "How does it relate to ACC Culverhouse?"

"I'm coming to that," said Madeleine Lefevre. "I contacted the forensic accountants from the Metropolitan Police trying to unravel the financial dealings of the late Ricky Gardiner. They are interested in Tony Fernandez and James Harlow. These names were used by Gardiner when working undercover. The flat where Gardiner died was rented in Harlow's name and sublet to Zena Gardjy. She confirmed that her landlord arrived on Tuesday evening and informed her he was staying for two nights. Warwickshire Police wanted Gardiner concerning a kidnapping in Royal Leamington Spa, and Wiltshire Police wanted him for the murder of former DS Terry Davis. Gardiner fled from a property he owned in Leek Wootton on Tuesday, the twenty-second of May and made for London. Where did he stay?"

"Are you asking me?" asked Culverhouse, "I thought we established this morning that I never met the man."

"That was what you claimed, yes," said Steve Nobbs, "perhaps we can jog your memory. The Met traced the properties rented by James Harlow and Tony Fernandez to Honor Oak Park and Croydon. Fingerprints collected from the Croydon flat belonged to Ricky Gardiner. The Met believes the empty flat was where Gardiner spent five nights after first reaching London. He left behind items of clothing and a mobile phone."

"A forensic officer was checking that phone when it rang," said Aysha Prasanna. "Imagine the surprise in Stafford when they spoke to Iris Collins at the third attempt to discover the identity of Contact B."

"Iris told them that the phone she held belonged to Tony Fernandez, aka Ricky Gardiner," said Madeleine Lefevre. "So, Staffordshire now had two-thirds of the puzzle. Sandra Plunkett and Ricky Gardiner."

"I told you Sandra could have known him," said Culverhouse. "The more I learn of that woman, the dirtier she looks. Who would have thought it?"

"What about the third person, Contact A?"

"Don't look at me! I never met Gardiner, and you can't prove I did."

"We'll park that subject for a while," said Madeleine. "We're waiting for further updates relating to the burner phones. First, I want to return to the hotel where you stayed. We re-examined CCTV images from the day you checked in. Your car entered the Novotel car park, and although we don't know the exact parking bay you chose, it's clear you selected a quiet corner not covered by the cameras. You said you sincerely hoped the car park CCTV was in operation. Strange that you picked such a vulnerable spot. Maybe you wanted to get something from the car before leaving the car park late on Tuesday evening?"

"Rubbish," said Culverhouse.

"We can't prove where you were in that missing hour

yet, but getting back to the hotel when you did was important, wasn't it? The concierge went off duty at eleven o'clock. I suggest you went to your room, read for a while, and dressed in the clothes we saw on the CCTV recording. You then slipped out to the car park via the rear door and collected the backpack from your car. Nobody would have seen you because it was pitch black. You crept along the far wall and darted through the entrance. We can guess what was in the backpack. We told you Gardiner died in a flat fire, but that didn't tell the complete story. Despite the fire damage, the autopsy showed he suffered blunt-force trauma to the back of the head. His attacker poured accelerants on the kitchen floor next to the body and set it alight as they left."

"You can't connect me to any of this," Culverhouse sneered. "You're making it up as you go along. I was in bed by eleven. Where's my motive? Why on earth would I want to murder a stranger?"

There was a knock at the door, and an IOPC officer entered with two folders. She handed them to Madeleine Lefevre.

"Bear with me for a second while I read this," she said.

Dominic Culverhouse tutted.

"Marcus White in Croydon; Jeff Gayle in Pinner; Bobby Beresford in Walthamstow. That may not be the complete list, but Gardiner used these names while working undercover. Using these false identities, he rented flats and sublet them. Some transactions from their bank accounts go back fifteen years. Forensic accountants have been working overtime. Ricky's father, George, died in 2001. Nobody queried what happened to his estate. Angie Gardiner didn't care. The evidence I see from Leek Wootton shows she was a wealthy woman. Ricky Gardiner inherited everything and eagerly awaited the sale of two expensive properties. However, George left his son a modest sum too, and Ricky transferred that money into a business account at another bank under the name GG Holdings. Tenants renting flats from Fernandez, Harlow and the others paid their monthly rent to GG Holdings. The rent money moved to Ricky's account twenty-four hours before the rent was due to pass to his real landlords. Nobody asked George or Ricky Gardiner about the constant credits and debits, which left the balance hovering around the eight hundred pounds balance showing when GG Holdings started trading in 2001."

"All very interesting," yawned Culverhouse, "how does any of this affect me?"

"Perhaps the second folder will shed light?" Madeleine replied with a smile. "This is my update on the burner phones."

Guy Templeman reckoned his concerns were justified. Dominic Culverhouse was as white as a sheet. Guy could see the cogs in his brain spinning, trying to fashion a way out of the vice-like grip by which Madeleine Lefevre held him.

"Staffordshire had no problem getting into the phone they recovered from Sandra Plunkett's home, as you know," said Madeleine. "Besides making calls to determine who the others were in the triangle, they checked the call logs. When were the phones used, and for how long? I agree that the most important call occurred on Tuesday, the twenty-second of May, between two thirty-eight and two forty-eight in the afternoon. Sandra Plunkett shared a conference call with Ricky Gardiner and the mysterious Contact A for six minutes, at which point Gardiner left the conversation. Sandra continued to talk to

Contact A for four minutes. Can you remember what you discussed?"

"I wouldn't know," snapped Culverhouse.

"Shall I tell you what I think?" asked Madeleine. "The kidnapping took place on the previous Friday afternoon. Gardiner fled the house where he held DI Ferris within one hour of leaving that conference call. The three of you argued. Sandra worried that she played a part in facilitating the kidnapping. Statements from Devizes and Leek Wootton confirm her Chief Constable instructed DI Ferris to leave phones and laptops at home when she attended the course at Ryton-on-Dunsmore. Gardiner ducked out of the conference call after six minutes, leaving you and Sandra to work out how to cover your tracks."

"You have a vivid imagination," said Culverhouse, "but no proof."

"I told you the initial allegations from Devizes convinced my superiors they were worth pursuing. We don't chase rainbows anymore than you. Like you, we pick the cases with the highest chance of success. We would be foolish to do otherwise. Ricky Gardiner was a fixer. He committed crimes for cash, and those eager beavers in the forensic accounting department of the Met came up trumps again. This case has proved a magnificent example of cooperation between police forces across the country. When the Staffordshire people searched for evidence to prove who bought that third phone, they found two cash withdrawals totalling five thousand pounds from Sandra's bank account. The first was on Friday the eleventh of May, and the second was on Wednesday the sixteenth."

"I shouldn't need to tell you how much a Chief Constable gets paid," said Culverhouse. "That sum wouldn't make a dent in her bank balance. There are dozens of reasons why Sandra might withdraw those amounts."

"Ricky Gardiner killed Terry Davis at around midnight on Sunday the thirteenth of May," said Madeleine. "Half the money upfront and the remainder on completion. I believe that's the way these things go. I wonder whether we might find similar transactions in your bank account. Ten thousand pounds seems a low figure for the murder of a policeman."

"When you get a search warrant, you can check," said Culverhouse, "I've nothing to hide."

"You mean that you believe you've covered your tracks sufficiently well that we won't find a money trail. We might not need it."

"If your financial demons from the Met had found anything in Gardiner's accounts with my name, you would have charged me by now. But, instead, you're still fishing."

"Our next clue came from Sandra Plunkett's bank account, as it happens," said Steve Nobbs, "there were two payments to Royal Mail for Special Delivery. Those payments guaranteed delivery of the cash by one pm the following day. On the twelfth of May, Ricky Gardiner was in Devizes. The money arrived at his hotel, and he signed for it. On Thursday, the seventeenth, Gardiner was in the Midlands stalking DI Ferris. The following day he kidnapped Suzie Ferris and took her to his late mother's home in Leek Wootton. I expect you can guess what happened mid-morning on Thursday. No comment? Ricky Gardiner signed for a second amount of two thousand five hundred pounds. Royal Mail provided us with copies of the signed documents. Proof positive that Sandra Plunkett knew Ricky Gardiner and paid him five thousand pounds for services rendered."

"Unless you go through a medium," said Culverhouse, "you can't ask Sandra whether she was repaying a debt or paying Gardiner to do something illegal on her behalf. I'm tired of repeating myself, but I didn't know Gardiner. I wasn't speaking with Sandra and Gardiner at any point."

"We can keep going if you wish," said Madeleine Lefevre. "I can't believe you imagine you'll walk away from this unscathed."

Dominic Culverhouse shrugged his shoulders.

"Gardiner travelled back to London by train soon after he completed the first half of the job you and Sandra Plunkett agreed," said Aysha Prasanna. "However, he needed to ensure the Leek Wootton property was ready for a guest. His late mother, Angie, hadn't lived there for years, and the place was in a poor state of repair. You can attest to that, can't you?"

Culverhouse didn't shrug on this occasion.

Guy Templeman spotted the tension in his colleague's jaw. The IOPC team were closing in for the kill.

"Your car is distinctive," said Steve Nobbs, "we know from the Oakley incident that you prefer to drive a prestige vehicle. We soon spotted your Lexus travelling on the M5 and the M42 on the evening of Thursday, the seventeenth of May. We confirmed the registration on ANPR. You drove from Hereford to Leek Wootton to deliver the cash in person, didn't you? Sandra risked leaving a trail using Royal Mail and divided her contribution into two amounts. You handed Ricky Gardiner five thousand pounds in notes. When he cleared out on Tuesday, he was careful not to leave incriminating evidence behind at 186 Woodman Lane."

"You wouldn't disclose the details of the conference call that Tuesday afternoon," said Madeleine. "Events that followed suggest the three of you argued as I suggested. I imagine Gardiner told you he would drop you both in it if he got caught. He was an expert in self-preservation. An undercover cop who can stay in control with a loaded gun in his mouth knows how to save his skin. Can you remember how you concealed the cash, so nobody knew what you were carrying? Of course, it was in a white jiffy bag you found lying around at home. It was the perfect size for that amount of cash. You took the precaution of ripping off the label with your name and address, but Ricky never handled the bag, did he? What did he do, ask you to leave it on the kitchen table? Your fingerprints were all over it."

"Ricky must have worn gloves when he removed the cash," said Steve Nobbs, "he placed the empty bag on the Welsh dresser in full view. Almost as if he wanted the police to find it."

Guy Templeman knew the game was up. Dominic was as guilty as sin. He could see it written across his face in big, bold letters.

"There's more," said Madeleine Lefevre.

Guy Templeman could tell she was enjoying this. He couldn't blame her. Since they took over from the old Independent Police Complaints Commission, Dominic would be one of the biggest fish the IOPC had landed.

"I believe the object you used to disable Gardiner was a fibreglass-handled club hammer, and the accelerants used were bottles of paint thinner and white spirit. A man answering your description paid cash for these three items on Monday lunchtime at the B&Q Extra store in Millennium Leisure Park. The checkout operator remembered the uniform."

"What have you got to say, Dominic?" asked Guy Templeman.

"Lawyer."

Chapter Ten

Friday, 8 June 2018 - the Crime Review Team office

"THAT DIDN'T TAKE LONG," said Luke as Gus and Lydia exited the lift.

"You need to ask the right questions, Luke," said Gus.

"I asked most of them," said Lydia, "From the list that you handed me just before we entered the gallery."

"I rest my case," said Gus. "Lydia can update her section of the Freeman Files while you take me through the backgrounds you've dug out for our London gang members. How far is Islington from Barking? Does anybody know?"

"A little over ten miles, guv," said Luke, "thirty minutes tops. Why do you ask?"

"One name in Mark Malone's burner phone was Mehmet Barking. Can you see a Mehmet on your list of potential gang members?"

"I've got a Mehmet Demir, forty-four. He's spent more time in prison than out since arriving in 1994. There's no mention of him ever living in Essex, though. He's either in Stratford or Belmarsh. Mark Allison was a casualty in the October 2013 turf war in Islington when our murder weapon first surfaced. It's probable Mehmet Demir fired the gun on that occasion."

"We need to double-check Mehmet was on the streets for both murders," said Gus, "who else do we have?"

"I had three names left after I'd eliminated gang members in prison or dead at the time of Mark Malone's murder, guv," said Luke. "Besides Demir, I found Hakan Turgut, thirty-five, arrested for his involvement in the Islington turf war but never charged. Turgut hasn't changed his ways, he's still a soldier, and this shooting wouldn't be out of character for him. Violence is his stock-in-trade, and although he's not known to have killed anyone, the level of violence has been increasing, based on his court appearances."

"They sound a pleasant group of lads," said Gus, "when did Hakan arrive on these shores?"

"Hakan was born in the UK, guv, and he's well worth a look. Finally, we have Emir Polat, thirty-six, who arrived in 2008. It makes you wonder what checks get carried out. Polat had a record as long as your arm before leaving Turkey. As soon as he arrived, Emir got involved with one of the Stratford crews. Emir Polat is more brain than brawn. He could have recruited Mark Malone; if Mark got involved in criminal activity."

"You're right to rein me in, Luke," said Gus. "By focussing on the customised BMW and wondering how Mark could have afforded it without being a crook, we're not looking to see if Mark became a victim for another reason. I reckon the weekend has come at the right time.

We'll pick up the trail on Monday when Neil is back to help. I need to get my thinking cap on while working on my allotment. It might pay to go through everything we've learned this week to check that one of our interviewees wasn't hiding something."

"Everything points to Mark Malone being guilty of something, guv," said Lydia looking up from her computer monitor.

"That's what worries me," said Gus, "there's one piece of that Saturday night jigsaw that doesn't fit at the moment."

"The JET garage?" asked Luke.

"That's right. We know Trefor Davies is methodical. The detectives learned of the altercation between the two BMW drivers in that initial investigation. Unfortunately, that row got passed off as a spat between two motorists. Patrick Boddington told us Mark said he didn't know the man banging on his window."

"That means it couldn't have been Emir or Mehmet," said Luke.

"Unless Mark had never had a face-to-face meeting with them," said Gus.

"Hang on, let's recheck the original murder file," said Luke. "I remember reading that there was no further CCTV coverage after the JET garage on the A4. Which was why nobody could confirm whether the grey 7-Series BMW or the black SUV followed Mark along the Beckhampton straight."

"What was stopping both vehicles from following him?" asked Gus.

"It's possible," said Luke. He kept flicking through the paperwork in the murder file. "Here we go. The camera position wasn't great."

"When is it ever?" asked Gus, "in fairness, they're more concerned with a boy racer filling up and driving off without paying than two drivers having a shouting match."

"There's no question this was Mark's car," said Luke. "Even though the tinted windows prevent us from seeing his face. The grey BMW must have stopped behind him, and the driver jumped out. This image shows the unknown male banging on Mark's window."

"Note his physical description, Luke. How tall do you reckon? Between six foot and six foot three?"

"Looking at how he's leaning over the car, guv, yes, he's at least six foot tall. Stocky, well-muscled and with short black hair. He could weigh fifteen stones, give or take. There's no way we can make out his features, though."

"Do you have a photograph of Mehmet Demir handy?" asked Gus.

"That's not Demir, guv," said Luke. "he's short, over-weight, hairy and has a dark complexion."

"This guy could hardly be any different," said Gus, "so, who is he? Could that be Hakan Turgut?"

Luke searched for a recent photograph of Turgut from police records.

"We can't be one hundred per cent sure with only a back view, guv, but it's a possibility."

"I agree," said Gus, "it's close enough. On the other hand, the garage CCTV never caught sight of anyone else in the grey BMW, did it?"

Luke shook his head.

"Also, the black SUV was never on the forecourt according to the evidence Patrick Boddington gave us," said Gus. "Patrick said that Mark told him the black SUV appeared behind him after he'd left the garage. In that last conversation after midnight, as Mark headed towards the

Devizes exit off the roundabout, there was no hint that two cars were chasing Mark into town."

"No, guv," said Luke, "and there's nobody to ask."

"Well, we can ask the BMW and SUV drivers. Unless there's another gang member we haven't identified yet, Turgut and Polat were driving."

"Which means our suspected killer, Mehmet Demir, was a passenger in one car," said Luke.

"What was it you said earlier about a face-to-face meeting?" asked Gus. "How could we find that out?"

"Did Patrick make a note of the burner phone number, guv?" asked Luke.

"That wasn't on my list of questions, Luke. You can't blame Lydia for that. Patrick gave us a fair amount of detail, though. We can ask him later about the number. Emir first rang Mark on the burner phone in February 2014, which suggests they had already met for Emir to hand over the phone."

"Why was Emir identified as Pompey in the burner phone, guv? He's a Stratford lad."

"Emir wouldn't be the first criminal to leave the big city and move to a port such as Portsmouth," said Gus. "If we stick with our smuggling theory as the reason behind Mark working with them, then Portsmouth is as good a port to bring the dogs through as any."

"Fair comment. If Neil were here, he'd suggest a football connection. Emir lived in London but might have supported Portsmouth."

"Based on my limited knowledge of the area and football, Luke, West Ham would get Neil's vote. But, no, I'd discount football and concentrate on the deep water cargo terminal."

"How would Emir even learn about Mark, guv? I can't see them mixing in the same circles."

"Let's chew this over for a while," said Gus. "If the gang decided it was profitable to bring valuable animals into the country, what did they need? An access point with less security than an airport or a major Southern port; Southampton, London, or Felixstowe. They selected Portsmouth, and they've got their dogs in the UK. Now what?"

"They needed customers, guv," said Luke.

"Would you buy a dog from Mehmet Demir?" asked Gus.

"I get you," said Luke, "the gang needed a middleman, someone people trusted. Mark fitted the bill. He loved animals and had a well-established pet shop in a city with a sizeable population."

"So we can assume Emir did the talking. He's the brains of the operation. I doubt we'll be able to find any trace of Emir in Bath after this time. It's a task you can give to the Hub. Please give it a low priority. I don't want any of us trawling through reams of paperwork. He could have driven to Bath or let the train take the strain. Either way, he would be in and out in daylight hours."

"You're thinking of a brief visit to discuss or dictate terms and another trip to drop off the burner phone. Why not at the dog shows?"

"Excellent idea," said Gus. "that gave the gang access to numerous pet shop owners under the same roof. Maybe the initial contacts happened there, and those who agreed to cooperate received their phone in a face-to-face meeting. Maybe Mehmet or Hakan delivered the phones."

"That makes sense," said Luke, "Emir sweet-talked the owners, told them there was money in it for them, and several go ahead. Then, when the hard men arrive with the phones, the owners get the message that there's no turning back."

"Can you tell me where Mehmet was in February 2014 when Emir made that first call to Mark Malone?"

"Belmarsh, guv. He got out at the end of June."

"That fits; his first call to Mark came in August. Something doesn't add up."

"Ah, Hakan Turgut," said Luke.

"If Mehmet was in Belmarsh, then who delivered Mark's phone? It couldn't have been Hakan. Mark didn't recognise him at the garage."

"We've only got Patrick's word for that, guv," said Luke.

"I stand corrected, Luke," said Gus, "but why would Patrick lie?"

"I can't see he had anything to gain; no, I agree," said Luke.

"Perhaps, Emir had someone else on the books while his enforcer, Mehmet, was in prison, or he travelled to Bath himself. The Hub might investigate that for us. Emir could have relatives in the city."

"Patrick might shed light on that," said Luke. "We can ask when we call regarding the burner phone."

"So, after chewing it over for a few minutes, where have we got to?" asked Gus. "We still have holes, but we've got a framework for the gang's master plan. They set up a network of pet shops across the south of the country that took dogs smuggled through Portsmouth. The gang used the burner phones a month to six weeks apart. That must have coincided with the frequency of arrivals at the port. On Friday, before Mark died, there were three conversations between Emir and Mark. That was unusual and pointed to a problem that Emir wanted to fix. On Saturday afternoon, there was just one call. Thanks to Patrick again, we believe

Mark felt threatened by the BMW and the SUV. That suggests that the talking ended. Mark hadn't done what they asked, and it wouldn't end well when they got hold of him. They caught up with him at the JET garage, but things had to wait until they were somewhere quieter. Fifteen minutes later, after a high-speed chase into Devizes, one car overtook Mark and slowed him enough for Mehmet Demir to get off six shots."

"A lot of fuss for a few posh puppies," said Lydia, who had finished updating the files.

"Thank you, Lydia," said Gus, "that's another question to add to the list for my time at the allotment. You're right. We're still missing something. At the moment, I can't see it. So let's forget work for today, get off home, enjoy the weekend, and we'll come back refreshed on Monday."

Luke and Lydia didn't need telling twice. They tidied their desks and headed for the lift together within five minutes. Gus got his thoughts on the day's interview into the files. Anything that produced a niggle while he was keying it in was something else to ponder once he got home.

As Gus saved his work ten minutes later, nothing had struck him as out of sync with his overall impression of the Malone case. Instead, he wondered if that fact alone suggested they'd missed something. Maybe he was overthinking things, or he was tired and should get off home.

The phone rang. Gus groaned. Why hadn't he left with the others?

"Freeman," he answered.

"Truelove, here. Can you drop into London Road as soon as possible?"

"I'll leave straight away, Sir," said Gus, "can you tell me what it's about?"

Obviously not, Gus thought, as the line was dead.

Ah well, late on a Friday afternoon, he only had forty-five minutes to wait to find out. Gus cleared his desk and made his way to the car park. Just as he feared, the traffic was horrendous in both directions on the road out of town. So why didn't anyone work on a Friday afternoon anymore? Had someone announced a four-and-a-half day week was compulsory, and he'd missed it?

It was approaching five o'clock when he pulled into the London Road car park. There was plenty of space for visitors. Nobody was daft enough to make an appointment when the weekend had already started.

Gus reached the steps to the front entrance. As he placed his foot on the first step, the door opened, and the rush for home began. It was apparent none of the office staff planned to work any overtime.

Vera Butler and Kassie Trotter descended the steps together. Vera's new home was only a few minutes' walk away. Kassie would catch a bus to Worton after visiting a supermarket to stock up on supplies. Gus hadn't been here since Wednesday and missed their conversations. Times were changing.

"How are my two favourite admin staff?" Gus asked, hoping that didn't sound insincere.

"We're fine, Mr Freeman," said Kassie, "although we can't say the same for others we could mention."

"The Acting Chief Constable will give you the gory details, Gus," said Vera. "Things don't stay settled for long in this place these days. Kassie blames you, of course, but I know you can't control how other people react. However, there's a correlation between your return to work and this constant upheaval."

Vera smiled at Gus and kissed him on the cheek before

joining Kassie and walking out of the car park onto London Road.

The number of civilians leaving the building thinned enough for Gus to get inside. He signed in at reception and took the stairs two at a time to the first floor. A familiar face met him outside the ACC's office.

"You received the call too?" asked Geoff Mercer, "I was ready to make my way home. I promised Christine I would be early on a Friday evening for a change. That's gone out of the window now. Let's get in to see him and get this over with."

"You've no idea what it's about either, Geoff?" asked Gus.

"I know what happened first thing today. I told you Kenneth postponed our regular morning meeting, didn't I?"

"You said you could put your feet up for an hour, was that it?" said Gus.

Geoff ignored him, knocked, and opened the door. Kenneth Truelove sat at his desk, looking pleased as punch. Gus wasn't sure how to take this unusual state of affairs. The ACC either stared out of his window or appeared to have a dark cloud overhead when he sat at his desk. The beaming grin he wore this afternoon was disturbing.

"Come in, sit yourselves down, Freeman," said the ACC. "Mercer, lock the door if you please. I don't imagine many people are out there to barge in on proceedings, but we don't get many opportunities to celebrate."

The ACC walked over to a filing cabinet Gus had never seen open. Of course, he knew the ACC did more than attend meetings and have his photo taken at various functions. Still, the idea that Truelove generated enough paperwork to fill a filing cabinet was alien.

"I have not had to get this out too often in the recent

past," he said. Gus and Geoff watched as a tray with half a dozen glasses appeared from the bottom drawer. Cut crystal goblets, Gus realised, not mere glasses. The ACC retrieved an unopened bottle of Scotch from the middle drawer.

"Is that the Isle of Jura?" asked Gus.

"It's always been a favourite of mine," said the ACC.

"What are we celebrating?" asked Gus, keeping his fingers crossed it was news from Portishead.

The ACC poured three generous measures and handed goblets to Gus and Geoff.

"Time to start using first names. Geoff knows this first piece of news already, and no doubt you'll be pleased to hear it too, Gus. I've waited a long time for the opportunity to sit in this seat with the powers of Chief Constable, even if only until they appoint a successor to Sandra Plunkett. I spoke with the PCC and explained what I planned to do and why. He had no objections. I called Peter Morgan to see me this morning and told him we no longer required his services."

"I'll drink to that," said Gus, "how did he take it?"

"As you might expect," said the ACC, "Morgan wanted to know why. I told him it was because he couldn't keep his mouth shut. As a result, we suffered five years of confidential matters leaking from London Road to Terry Davis in Marbella via Monty Jennings. Whoever takes over as Chief Constable deserves staff at every level held to higher standards. I hope that applies to my replacement, too, when the time comes."

"Did he threaten to appeal to a higher authority?" asked Gus. "Peter always prided himself on having the ear of the Chief Constable, and I can imagine he would stress that you were just temporary."

Kenneth smiled again. He was having fun.

"I planned this for a while, Gus. Give me credit. Young Kassie Trotter complained more than once that Peter made inappropriate comments, you know?"

"Her embonpoint?" asked Gus.

"Her hearts and love bird tattoos?" asked Geoff.

"Exactly that," said the ACC, "and Kassie found several other ladies to offer similar complaints. I told Morgan it would be best if he left at the end of the month without making a fuss. If he persisted, I'd bring the other matters to the PCC's attention. I received his written resignation this afternoon."

"Happy days," said Geoff.

"I imagine there's more to come?" asked Gus.

"More news and more whisky," said Kenneth, getting up to replenish their goblets. "The IOPC chief investigator, Madeleine Lefevre, contacted me an hour ago. The preliminary meeting at Portishead went better than we could have hoped. She has told her superiors that Dominic Culverhouse's case must proceed to a gross misconduct hearing and that criminal charges should follow in due course."

"Fantastic news," said Gus. "All week, I've wondered how that weasel might get himself off the hook. Did the Met uncover new evidence? How did they pin something on him at last?"

"Ms Lefevre has promised to send me a full report of the meeting. I'll let you both read it in due course. In summary, Culverhouse looked to have got away with the hit-and-run. However, Sandra Plunkett's admission of her past error of judgement gave him a chance to sully her reputation further. Culverhouse blamed everything on her and swore blind he was too drunk to drive. Just the type of low trick you expect from the man."

"How did the IOPC connect him to Gardiner, Terry

Davis's murder, Suzie's kidnapping and so forth?" asked Gus.

"That was teamwork, Gus, just what we want to see. Detectives in Warwickshire and West Mercia Police found evidence that chipped away at Culverhouse's insistence that he had no case to answer. All the while, the forensic accountants at the Met peeled back layer upon layer of the mask hiding Gardiner's financial affairs."

"Did Culverhouse kill Ricky Gardiner?" asked Gus.

"He did," said the ACC, "whacked him over the head with a hammer, carried him upstairs to the flat, doused him with accelerant, and struck a match as he left. Madeleine told me they had a few holes in the timeline to fill in when Culverhouse cried for a lawyer. Since then, the Met Police found an Uber driver who carried Culverhouse from Greenwich to Honor Park after ten o'clock. The driver confirmed his passenger carried a backpack. The last thing Ms Lefevre learned was that a CCTV camera outside the General Napier pub caught sight of Culverhouse two hours earlier. He wasn't wearing a hoodie or backpack, but he was keeping watch at the pub where Gardiner spent his last evening."

"That report sounds fascinating reading," said Gus, "as a rule, I don't concern myself with the follow-up to a case, but this time I'll make an exception. Are you sure you don't have any juicy titbits you can let me have?"

"Are you offering a *quid pro quo*?" asked the ACC.

"I assume you want to hear how we're doing with the Malone case? I warned you not to expect an easy ride on that one. Although I can offer *something* in return."

"Her Ladyship naively kept the phone she used when speaking with Culverhouse and Gardiner. Sandra also paid for a guaranteed cash delivery with funds from her bank account. Culverhouse made several mistakes when forced to make split-second decisions in the final few days. He paid cash for tools he took with him when he killed Gardiner, but the B&Q employee remembered the police uniform. It might surprise you that Culverhouse visited 186 Woodman Lane the day before DI Ferris reached there. He reckoned without Gardiner's aptitude for self-preservation. Culverhouse put the blood money in a jiffy bag to pay Gardiner for his services. Gardiner left that jiffy bag covered in Culverhouse's prints in full view for the Warwickshire detectives to find."

Gus finished the last mouthful of his amber nectar.

"The perfect companion to celebrate a long-awaited successful outcome," he said.

"Over to you," said Kenneth Truelove, "what have you got?"

"A gang of Turkish Cypriots from Stratford smuggled dogs into the country through Portsmouth," said Gus. "We believe the gang recruited Malone and others at dog shows across the South. Luke Sherman's identified three gang members so far. All three were at the JET garage on the A4 at midnight on the night of the murder. Malone drove towards Devizes, chased by the grey 7-Series BMW and a black SUV. The man who shot Malone was a passenger in the SUV."

"Excellent," said Kenneth, "when can I expect an arrest?"

"I've no idea," said Gus, "I still don't know what's so profitable about smuggling a few hundred puppies. Even if they're an exotic breed Beyoncé once owned, it's a niche market, and organised crime gangs don't get involved in fads. They want things that deliver a steady income stream."

"Anything else?" asked the ACC.

"Malone's mother swears her son loved animals. So why get involved in a trade where the death rate for the smuggled dogs is high? It does not compute, Captain."

"You'll sort it, Gus," said Geoff, "if you want my opinion, the only thing those thugs would deal in were narcotics, not exotics."

"We'll start again with fresh minds on Monday," said Gus, "Neil Davis returns to work, so we'll have an extra pair of hands. We're missing something. I'll give it thought over the weekend, and then we'll go again."

"I'll let you know when the IOPC report is available, Gus," said the ACC. "I promise not to call you here on Monday morning. However, it would help if you got another success under your belt as soon as possible. Then, when they appoint our next Chief Constable, every feather in my cap increases my chance of securing that early retirement."

"We think you're doing a cracking job in your temporary position, Sir," said Geoff Mercer, "Gus and I should start getting a petition together. Either you get the job, or they persuade you to stay as the new Chief's right-hand man for two years. Just to let them find their feet. This force needs stability."

"I knew it was a colossal mistake giving you a drink, Mercer," said Kenneth Truelove, "the last thing my wife wants to hear is a postponement of my retirement."

"Unlock the door, Geoff," said Gus, "I'm going home. Phone Christine; I'm sure she'll collect you if she wants you home at a reasonable hour. Kenneth here is fine for two or three hours. After that, he can decide whether to call a taxi or brew himself a strong pot of coffee. Your wife is at her Pilates class tonight, isn't she?"

"Yes, Gus, you're right. I'll opt for coffee. See you sometime next week. Have a pleasant weekend."

"Thanks," said Gus, "well, there's one thing we can guarantee."

"What's that?" asked Geoff.

"Even if we have a lousy weekend, it will be better than Dominic Culverhouse's."

Chapter Eleven

Saturday, 9 June 2018

"ARE you getting out of bed today?" asked Suzie.

"I blame Kenneth Truelove," said Gus, "and I plead the fifth."

"The fifth what?"

"Tumbler of whisky I drank last night. The ACC kicked things off at five o'clock with his Isle of Jura. I drove home after the second at six o'clock."

"You shouldn't have. All you needed to do was call me. I would have collected you from London Road and got you home."

Even with a thick head, Gus didn't miss that one. Suzie called it home, not back here, or something impersonal. Gus tried to recall where he'd put those spare keys for safe-keeping.

"If you can drag yourself to the shower, I'll cook breakfast," said Suzie.

Gus watched her walk to the bedroom door.

"There's a shirt in the wardrobe," he said. "The postman often arrives early on a Saturday, and the sausages I bought last week spit more than the other brand. Of course, I'm only thinking of your delicate skin."

Suzie looked in the wardrobe.

"Are blue and white the only colour options in your shirts?"

"I'm a man. How many more do I need? Looking at the extreme left-hand side, you'll find shirts Tess bought me. I had to wear them once to be polite. You can use those with impunity. I don't mind if they get spattered with hot fat."

"Get in that shower, Freeman," said Suzie, grabbing a corner of the duvet and whipping it off the bed.

Gus opened one eye to see Suzie wearing the pink shirt he'd worn for his consultant interview. It looked better on Suzie.

"I'm going," said Gus, "remind me again why I let you in when you turned up on my doorstep at nine last night?"

"If I do, you'll never get in that shower," said Suzie. "You must be hungry after that exercise. We both need a hearty breakfast. Then, once I've got you feeling human again, I'm driving back to the farm to ride. You can prepare lunch, and we'll spend the afternoon on the allotment."

"I planned to work through the Malone case to determine what we've missed."

"I understand that darling," said Suzie, "but you have to remember, I've only been back at work since Wednesday. They wouldn't let me do more than half-days, and my brain needed extra stimulation. Believe it or not, I'm a detective. I might provide a lightbulb moment."

Gus strolled into the en suite bathroom and turned on

the shower. Two heads were better than one. If he could get his head to stop thumping, the Freeman-Ferris combination might prove a winner.

After breakfast, Suzie showered and dressed. Gus sat with his second cup of coffee and waited for her to emerge from the bedroom.

"What time will you be back?" he asked.

"If I say two o'clock, can you prepare us something to eat at the allotment? The sooner you review this case, the better. We'll have a working lunch."

"I thought you'd sit and watch me work with the file on your lap," said Gus.

"You are dense sometimes, Gus," laughed Suzie, "I grew up on a farm. My father might farm livestock, but my mother grew the fruit and vegetables we needed. My brother and I were handling a rake and a hoe before we went to school. I know my onions."

Gus groaned and followed Suzie to her car.

"We've got a grand day for it," she said.

They shared a long kiss before Suzie got behind the wheel of her GTI.

"Was that for my benefit or the neighbours?" asked Gus.

"Bugger the neighbours, that was for me. I've got three hours before I see you again."

Gus stood on the doorstep and watched Suzie perform a speedy three-point turn in his neat driveway. Then, with a defiant bark, the GTI surged towards the entrance and disappeared up the lane towards Worton.

Gus forgot to wave Suzie on her way. He assessed the work needed to put all the small stones scattered in her wake back in their rightful place. The exuberance of youth.

The third cup of coffee did the trick, and Gus felt

human enough to cross jobs from his to-do list. He loaded the breakfast things into the dishwasher and wandered to the lounge. The Greg Allman album was still on the turntable. Suzie brought it with her last night. Gus returned it to its precious sleeve and left it on the stack of favourites he rarely went a week without playing. Gus knew better than to leave it in the hallway so Suzie could take it home again when she left.

When he drank whisky as he had last night, there were artists he listened to that seemed to fit the music and his mood. Suzie had reckoned John Lee Hooker wasn't the proper background track for two lovers who hadn't seen one another for a week. So, One Bourbon, One Scotch, One Beer was the last tune for the late bluesman. They settled on the sofa together, and Gus let her choice of southern rock music flow over him. If he tired of the old-style blues in his later years, then Allman would be a worthy companion.

Suzie had left London Road soon after five yesterday afternoon, and they'd missed one another on the steps by a few minutes. Gus told her the news about Dominic Culverhouse. It elated Suzie. That entire episode could get forgotten in time.

As for Peter Morgan getting the elbow, Suzie thought it long overdue.

"Morgan was a creep," she said, "with an exceedingly high opinion of himself. He tried it on with me once, but I gave him short shrift. Vera was his favourite, though. He couldn't believe it when you arrived from nowhere and stole her from under his nose."

"Was that the way he saw it?" Gus had asked. "I didn't realise."

Not long after that, they'd stopped talking.

GUS'S REVERIES ENDED, and he remembered that he'd need supplies if he were preparing a picnic lunch. When did he last go shopping? He couldn't remember. A swift inventory of the kitchen told him that the supermarket trip he'd planned was still overdue. The driveway would have to keep looking as if a bomb had hit it. Gus grabbed his car keys and headed for the front door.

Before he left, he darted back into the bedroom and rooted through his jacket pockets without luck. In time Gus found the spare set of keys behind the cafetiere and placed them on the hall table. He didn't want to appear to be taking too much for granted, so he left them half-hidden behind a vase of dried flowers.

Gus sat in the old Focus and thought of what he had done. It was no good. He got out, opened the front door and grabbed the dried flowers. Gus threw them in the green recycling bin when he got outside again. He made a mental note to add fresh flowers to the supermarket list of things to buy.

It was noon before he returned to the bungalow. Saturday morning shopping was never sensible; too many others had the same bright idea. Gus was ready to get lunch with everything stored away in the fridge, the chest freezer or the wine rack.

The flowers in the hallway were an imaginative touch. They caught your eye when you came through the door.

Gus began work with renewed energy. Suzie drove through the gateway at a quarter to two. Gus waited in the kitchen with his handiwork. Suzie would soon spot it and fine-tune the menu if he'd forgotten anything. The allotment could wait fifteen minutes for things to be perfect.

"Have you missed me?" she asked, kissing Gus on the cheek.

"Far too busy," said Gus, "did you enjoy your ride?"

"It always cheers me up and makes me hungry," said Suzie, "this food looks terrific. Are you ready to go? We'll walk along the lane to the allotment. It's too nice a day to sit in a stuffy car."

Gus couldn't agree more. He collected his case notes and joined Suzie in the hallway. She had stowed their lunch in a bag for life and was itching to leave.

Gus glanced towards the vase of flowers. They looked great and gave off a pleasant aroma.

The spare keys still peeked out from behind the vase. Too soon, perhaps?

"Where is everyone?" asked Suzie when they reached the allotments. "I thought this place would be a hive of activity today."

"Maybe they've done the hard graft and decided the weather was too good to miss," said Gus.

"Where's your old friend, Bert? He's always here."

Gus opened the garden shed and brought out the chair for Suzie. An upturned seed tray would suffice for the odd moments when he stopped work.

"Make yourself as comfortable as you can," he said, "I'll bring you up to speed on what's happened since last weekend."

Gus told Suzie about the dreadful accident in Saskatoon. He wanted to see Bert back on the patch of land next door too. But these things follow an uncertain course. Bert Penman might turn up later this afternoon and carry on with his weeding and thinning, or he may never recover from the blow. Gus remembered how hard Tess's death hit him when he was the best part of, twenty-five years younger than Bert.

"Do you think the Reverend is with him?" asked Suzie.

"That's a possibility," said Gus, "Although I've seen her arrive here later on a Saturday. The church still gets the occasional wedding, and sermons don't write themselves. So once Clemency's ready for her busiest day of the week, she often appears out of the blue and potters on her plot for an hour. She finds it therapeutic."

"When are you visiting Bert?" asked Suzie.

"I promised Clemency I'd drop by when things were quiet."

"We'll both go tomorrow," said Suzie, "otherwise, you'll keep putting it off."

Gus started hoeing. There was plenty to do now without Bert's input. He looked across at his friend's patch of ground, and although it looked in far better condition than his, there were still a few weeds that needed attention.

"I'll see to Bert's housekeeping," said Suzie, "you concentrate on your rows of plants. Right, take me through this interview you had with Jenny Malone."

"It felt genuine," said Gus, "Mark's father left when their son reached eighteen. Jenny ran her own business, and Mark moved out at twenty."

"What did his father do for a living?"

"Gerry Malone's an architect."

"And Jenny's business?"

"An employment agency that she runs from home."

"Your notes suggest you're too concerned with where Mark got the money to pay for his customised BMW."

"Well, wouldn't you be? A young man, working as a pet shop manager, driving that car. It didn't sit right with me."

Gus carried on working. Suzie continued to read for a while and started weeding Bert Penman's allotment.

"Mark loved animals," said Suzie.

Gus was further up his patch of ground and realised Suzie had said something. He straightened up and looked towards her.

"Sorry," she said, "I was thinking out loud. Jenny Malone made a point about that. So did Patrick Bodding-ton. Does it fit with being in league with a gang smuggling dogs into the country?"

"Luke's research suggested there was enough money for organised crime gangs to milk it for all it was worth. So we concluded that they recruited Mark at a dog show, and he made enough money from the deal to buy his fancy motor. So what do you think we've missed?"

"You know I started at Pony Club as soon as I was old enough to sit in a saddle," said Suzie. "I've adored horses all my life. Can you imagine me helping someone bring ponies over from the continent in horrendous conditions to give me the cash to upgrade my GTI?"

"Never in a million years," said Gus, laying his hoe on the ground. "We must go back to something that happened before he met Emir Polat and the others. Something that enabled Mark to buy the car."

"Once you've done that, you might discover the real motive for his murder," said Suzie.

"Can we stop work for a while and enjoy this lunch I prepared?" asked Gus, "I put two small bottles of Chardonnay in the cooler. Your intuition might have given us a fresh lead to pursue on Monday. That's an excuse for a little celebration."

"I didn't see a corkscrew in the bag," said Suzie, unpacking the food.

"Just as well I bought the screw-top variety then," said Gus, "I'm no wine snob."

After they devoured the lunch and polished off the wine, it was time to resume work on the allotment. The church clock struck six o'clock before they felt ready to call it a day.

"We've made a start," said Gus, "another stint tomorrow, and I'll be happy."

"We're calling on Bert Penman tomorrow, don't forget," said Suzie. "His well-being is more important than that of a few plants. Anyway, those clouds hold rain. We won't need to water this evening, and tomorrow could be a washout. So why don't we pack away your tools, get back home for a shower, and change out of these dirty clothes?"

"Will you need to borrow my shirt again?" asked Gus.

"I brought clean clothes in the car," said Suzie. "This gardening lark develops a thirst. No wonder Bert is such a regular visitor to the pub. I vote for a meal in the Lamb and an early night."

"Motion seconded," said Gus, "and carried."

Sunday, 10 June 2018

GUS WAS AWAKE EARLY and felt far better than he did yesterday.

The Lamb had been a superb idea of Suzie's yesterday evening. Their food was excellent, the cold lagers hit the spot, and the locals were keen to chat. Any planned early night was soon a memory.

Gus and Suzie had sat in the beer garden. The clouds Suzie identified as rain-bearing still gathered over the village. At ten o'clock at night, they delivered that sticky, uncomfortable feeling that often precedes a thundery downpour. The deluge came at three this morning, one reason Gus woke so early. The storm did little to lower the temperature.

Irene North had been the first person to leave the bar's heat and come outside to join them last night.

"I went to see Bert today, Mr Freeman," she began, "he's depressed. So I took fresh fruit round to him and a half-bottle of his favourite Scotch. What a terrible thing to have happened, wasn't it?"

"Yes, Irene," said Gus, "we're planning to call on him tomorrow."

"Suzie Ferris, isn't it?" asked Irene, turning her attention to Suzie. "I was at school with your father. He was younger than me, of course."

Delicately put, Irene, Gus had thought.

"That's me," said Suzie. "Dad often talks about when Frank worked on our farm. We were sorry for your loss."

Fifteen-all, thought Gus. No doubt John Ferris had to check the contents of his barns to see if nothing went missing while Frank was there. Frank North was a rascal.

Irene North soon drank up and walked home. The pub door opened, and Clemency Bentham came out with a tall glass with several ice cubes.

"A slimline tonic, before you ask, Gus," she said, "it took me two days to recover from that whisky you gave me the other evening."

"That was medicinal. By the way, we're both visiting Bert tomorrow," said Gus.

"Wonderful," said Clemency. "You've been busy on the allotment, too; I dropped by at eight this evening. I wanted to harvest lettuce, spring onions and radishes to add to my salads this week."

"Did you cycle here tonight?" asked Gus.

"No, I walked," said Clemency. "I cycled seven miles this afternoon while I composed my sermon. I embrace technology coming from the background I did, and I record it as I ride, then I type it into a file tomorrow morning ready for evensong."

Clemency chatted with them for a further ten minutes before leaving. Gus and Suzie watched the world go by until the landlord called time.

"Your turn to cook breakfast," said Suzie, raising her head from the pillow for the first time this morning. Gus knew any chance of another daydream was out of the question.

"Shower first, and then I'll get cracking," said Gus.

"Wait for me," said Suzie.

"I'LL GET BRUNCH THEN, shall I?" asked Gus two hours later. Suzie nodded and turned over. Gus headed for the bathroom. Twenty minutes later, they sat together in the kitchen, eating breakfast.

"What are your plans for the day after we've visited Bert?" asked Suzie.

"We could pick up where we left off on the allotment," suggested Gus. "Unless you want to drive somewhere, dodge these rain showers while we take a walk, and then visit a restaurant."

"Highly preferable to the other weekend," said Suzie giving a tiny shiver.

"Do you want to discuss that now?" asked Gus, "We've avoided it so far this weekend. I didn't want to spoil the mood on Friday night. So what was your reaction to the news last Monday? Who told you about Sandra Plunkett's death?"

"Geoff Mercer called in the evening and told me the full story," said Suzie, "I was at home when the news broke around lunchtime. They said then that it was a tragic accident. I never liked the woman and wanted her arrested for what she'd done, but I never wished her dead. That was a sad end."

"You were snooping around at London Road when news of Ricky Gardiner's death got released, weren't you? Kassie and Vera spotted you outside Geoff's office."

"I was crawling up the walls with boredom sitting at home," said Suzie. "When Geoff told me Gardiner was dead, I felt empty. My day in court was snatched away from me. There was nothing I could do. I'd never get the chance to watch him get the sentence he deserved."

"There are sure to be repercussions following the Culverhouse affair," said Gus. "A talented prosecution lawyer will dig out his past misdemeanours. Terry Davis's reputation might get a deserved polish at last. The more wrongdoing they can pile on the charge list, the better."

"I never met Culverhouse," said Suzie, "but hiding the hit-and-run, ordering Terry Davis's murder, and killing Ricky Gardiner merits more than a life sentence. It would be bad enough if he were a common criminal, but this guy was touting to be a Chief Constable. Just imagine how the media will spin it. What Culverhouse did was despicable."

"We can draw a line under that now and move on. London Road will have a new Police Surgeon in July and possibly a new Chief Constable. As for the Crime Review Team, Neil's back in the morning, and Alex is on the road to recovery. Fingers crossed, there's no relapse, and he'll rejoin us in early July. The same week as Blessing Umeh."

"What a splendid name. Who is she, and where is she from?" asked Suzie.

"Blessing was the DS in Leamington Spa who worked with DI Andy Carlton when they discovered your GTI. Andy rated his DS highly, and when her parents moved to Bath, Blessing wanted to come with them. Her father is taking up a post at Bath University in September. The ACC snatched her from under the noses of Avon & Somerset."

"If they haven't moved south yet, where will Blessing stay in the interim?" asked Suzie.

"Lydia's place would be my first choice, as they hit it off straight away that day. Alex might not appreciate Lydia getting a flatmate, though. Vera Butler could offer to put her up for a month or two. I'm not sure what Blessing would make of Kassie Trotter, and I don't know what Kassie's situation is in that house in Worton. I've stopped outside, watched her dart through the hedge, and heard a door slam. I've no idea whether she's renting a room or a self-contained flat. Do you know?"

"It's near the pub, isn't it? I've heard Kassie say she rents a room from a mate from school, but she doesn't give much away. One thing's certain; she's better off than if the ACC hadn't saved her from a life on the streets."

"We still haven't decided what's happening later," said Gus. "Come on, let's visit Bert and offer our condolences. Why don't we persuade him to spend an hour at the allotment? If we can get him out of the house, it might kick-start his recovery. If nothing else, it will take his mind off the funerals next Friday, even if only for an hour."

"I agree," said Suzie. "That's settled. We'll spend time with Bert, then drive somewhere for a meal. I'd better leave before eight to get my stuff ready for work in the morning. You're right. Next Friday will be awful for Bert, unable to get there."

"Clemency and Irene plan to spend time with him

throughout the day," said Gus. "I couldn't commit to a time when I spoke with Clemency. Who knows what Friday will bring?"

Gus persuaded Suzie to let him drive to Bert's house. He didn't fancy trying to get Bert into her GTI.

It felt strange knocking on his old friend's door. They must have spoken a thousand times on the allotment, but neither man had ever visited the other's home.

"It's open. Come on in, Mr Freeman," said Bert, "I saw you walking up the garden path."

"Why does Bert need an allotment?" whispered Suzie, "heaven knows how much land he has at the back, but there's more than enough here."

"I'm guessing this front garden was Cora's domain," said Gus, "lots of different bushes and flowering shrubs provide ground cover. Not the worst view to have out of your front window, is it? Tess would have approved."

They found Bert sitting in a high-backed solid-looking chair by the fireplace. The cushions softened the blow. His stick lay idle on the nearby table.

"I'm sorry it took so long to get to see you, Bert," Gus said.

"I understand, Mr Freeman. You're a busy man," said Bert. "I've met you, too, haven't I, Miss? You were with Mr Freeman when they found poor Frank North's body."

"That's right, Mr Penman," said Suzie, giving the old man's hand a gentle squeeze. "I'm Suzie Ferris."

"We did the weeding for you, Bert," said Gus, "Suzie and I worked on the allotment for four hours yesterday. There are still a few things that need seeing to, but we weren't sure what to do first."

"Gus tells me if he gets stuck, he only has to look up and call across to you, and you have the answer," said Suzie.

"I haven't been along there for a while," said Bert, "not since it happened. I still can't take it in, Mr Freeman. My David was such a careful driver. Forty years without an accident. What day is it today?"

"Sunday, Bert," said Gus, "didn't you hear the church bells earlier?"

"I can't miss the darn things when I'm on the allotment," said Bert. "My Cora wanted to live closer to the church so she could hear them, but I persuaded her to move here, on the edge of the village."

"How long have you lived here, Mr Penman?" asked Suzie.

"Sixty-two years, Miss," said Bert.

"If we take you to the allotment in the car, Bert, can you tell us what jobs need tackling?"

"Will that Ford Focus of yours stand the extra weight, Mr Freeman?" asked Bert.

Suzie offered him an arm to help him get out of the chair. She needn't have bothered. Bert had his stick in his hand and was halfway to the front door.

With Bert safely seated outside his shed, Gus and Suzie did as Bert ordered for the next hour. The fresh air and the company worked their magic. Bert would have a long hard road to travel before he could manage his loss. Gus knew it was likely that he'd never get over it totally, but this afternoon had been the first step to a kind of normal.

Gus drove back to Bert's just after three o'clock, and while he chatted to Bert, Suzie put the kettle on.

"Tea for me, Miss," he said, "two sugars, but don't tell the Reverend. She's been nagging me to join her on a diet."

"The Reverend cycles everywhere of late," said Gus, "I can't see her persuading you to join her, Bert. I reckon your allotment keeps you fit enough without additional exercise."

"Her heart's in the right place," said Bert as Suzie returned with two coffees and a sweet tea. "She's been a blessing these past few days."

"We visited the Lamb last night," said Gus, "the place wasn't what it was. The landlord wondered how long he could survive without his best customer."

"Get away with you, Mr Freeman," said Bert, "I'll be back in there for a pint of cider tomorrow. I've spent too long feeling sorry for myself. We didn't sort out every problem there today, and nature has its way of healing. I've tinkered in my garden, but it's not the same."

"We admired your front garden as we came up the path," said Suzie, "do you have much land at the back of the house?"

"I've got apple trees at the bottom of the garden," said Bert, "and my greenhouses on either side of my lawn. There's no room for much else."

"Do you ever run out of things to do?" asked Suzie.

"When I do, that will be the day I turn up my toes," said Bert. "So, I need to keep busy. I'm not done yet."

Gus and Suzie thought it was time to make a move. Bert Penman would ride out this particular storm in his life.

"I'll drop round to see you later in the week, Bert," said Gus, "who knows, I might wrap up this latest case and have an hour on the allotment one evening. Perhaps we can pop into the Lamb after we finish and have a drink together?"

"Of course, Mr Freeman," said Bert, "anything to keep the place running for the community. We should do our bit."

They left Bert in his high-backed chair and walked back to the car.

"Mission complete," said Suzie.

"Well, the first stage anyway," said Gus, "so, where do you want to eat?"

"Let's drive to the Waggon & Horses at Harrington End."

Gus recalled his first kiss with Vera.

"Been there, done that," he said, "I've driven past the Fox & Hounds several times and never stopped for a meal. So why not try somewhere different?"

"It's got an excellent reputation," said Suzie, "fingers crossed the place isn't busy."

They didn't have long to wait for a table, and sitting outside with a cold beer on a warm evening was no hardship. Two hours later, Gus swung the Focus into the driveway of the bungalow and parked beside Suzie's GTI.

"We've had a grand weekend, haven't we," she said.

"Rounded off with a fine meal, too," said Gus, "another name to add to our list of restaurants we enjoy. It's almost eight. I guess you'll be on your way?"

"I need to use your bathroom first, if I may?" said Suzie, dancing on the doorstep.

Gus opened the door, and Suzie disappeared. He wandered into the lounge.

When Suzie returned, she'd collected several clothing items from the bedroom, including his pink shirt, and looked ready to go.

"I'll get the washing on when I get back to the farm," she explained. "What did you do with my Greg Allman?"

Gus pointed to the stack of favourites, and Suzie nodded in appreciation. It appeared the album was staying.

Gus saw Suzie to the door, and they kissed goodnight.

"I hope your first day back goes well," said Gus.

"Good luck with your case," said Suzie, "I hope our

joint effort yesterday helps you make progress. Say hello to Neil for me, too. I'll call you tomorrow night. Bye."

Suzie made her customary noisy exit from the driveway, and Gus closed the front door. Crikey, it was quiet here without her.

As Gus passed the hall table, the scent of fresh flowers caught his attention.

The spare set of keys had gone.

Chapter Twelve

Monday, 11 June 2018

WHEN GUS DROVE into the car park on Monday morning, he realised Geoff Mercer had to sort out more spaces. Neil Davis was already here and parked next to Lydia's red Mini. Luke would be out of luck once Alex returned, and then there was Blessing Umeh.

It wasn't only the car parking that needed attention; the CRT required desks, chairs, laptops, and extra mugs in the restroom. Gus hadn't imagined a few successful cold cases would generate so much bureaucracy. He hoped Geoff saw these matters as his problem and didn't delegate it to the mere consultant.

"Good morning, guv," said Neil when Gus exited the lift.

"Welcome back, Neil," said Gus, "how's Melody?"

"She's gone to her mother's this morning, guv. I'm driving there after work. Finger's crossed, we don't have late finishes this week. Melody's improving daily, but she couldn't face being alone."

"Did you have a quiet relaxing weekend, guv?" asked Lydia.

"It had its moments," he replied, "and how's Alex?"

"He's getting stronger, guv. I'm still optimistic about a return to work in early July. There will be days when he feels he needs the pills to get through the pain, but he has the tools to overcome those urges. Alex's support system is robust. Between us, his family and me, that is, we won't let him slip up now. He's come too far."

"Good to hear," said Gus. "We miss him. We missed you too, Neil."

"London Road kept me in touch, guv," said Neil. "DS Mercer rang with the news of the Chief Constable. Amelia called to say Peter Morgan got sacked on Friday, although she wasn't sure why."

"Loose lips," said Gus. "He leaked the gossip that reached your Dad. The ACC felt he needed to send the troops a message while sitting in the hot seat."

"Peter Morgan and Amelia are related," said Lydia, "maybe he didn't make inappropriate comments to her in case her Dad belted him."

"Oh, right," said Neil. "Geoff Mercer called Friday night to tell me about Culverhouse and Gardiner. Dad always reckoned Culverhouse was rotten. I wish I could tell him he was right, and he will get his comeuppance."

Luke Sherman was last through the door. The full CRT compliment, for now, was in the building. Gus wanted to get things started.

"I gave the Malone case a lot of thought at the weekend. I kept thinking we missed something, and I may have stumbled on it. We'll re-interview Jenny Malone and Patrick Boddington today. In addition, we need to speak to Julian Drummond and any show dog owners Mark Malone often contacted. Lydia, can you analyse those detailed phone records again and select a handful? That should be enough to learn the scale of this smuggling operation. By the end of today, I hope we'll understand the motive behind the murder."

"I'll chase Drummond," said Lydia, "he promised us a list of people Mark might have visited on his way to Newbury."

"Who's going with you today, guv," asked Luke.

"I'd like you with me, Luke. Neil, you can read through the Freeman Files, familiarise yourself with the case, and help Lydia fix up interviews. When Luke and I return, you can give us your impressions of what we've learned. A fresh look at the evidence will confirm or deny the niggle I've suffered these past few days. These follow-up interviews should offer a fresh perspective."

Luke called Jenny Malone and Patrick Boddington to tell them they were on their way.

Gus rang Geoff Mercer and asked whether there was enough in the budget for the additional items the CRT needed in the coming weeks.

Gus could still hear the laughter after ending the call.

Perhaps the new Police Surgeon wouldn't miss the odd item from Peter Morgan's office. There was little point considering Sandra Plunkett's furniture. It would be far too grand for the Old Police Station, and the ACC would have removed anything worth having already.

"Do you have a particular line of enquiry to follow this morning, guv," asked Luke as they reached the car park.

"I spent time with DI Ferris on Saturday afternoon, running through the interviews we carried out. Suzie thought it suspicious that Mark Malone, a devout animal-lover, went into business with people such as Emir Polat. To her, it suggested Mark didn't rely on the gang's money to pay for his BMW. This morning, I hope to learn the truth. Jenny and Patrick either lied to us directly or by omission."

Jenny Malone answered the door with little enthusiasm when they reached Combe Down. Gus didn't think she enjoyed having her morning interrupted. So he started in with his questions before she had time to sit.

"When my colleague and I came to see you last week," said Gus, "you mentioned your husband, Gerry. How old is he now?"

"Sixty-six," said Jenny.

"Gerry was twelve years older than you when you married. I imagine he was well-established in his profession. He was an architect, you said."

"Gerry worked for a major construction firm. He earned good money."

"When did you go into business? This employment agency you run from home, was that in existence thirty years ago?"

"I worked as an office temp when I met Gerry," said Jenny. "I planned to stay home with Mark until he started playschool and then resume work. Gerry suggested I combine temping with the agency. After two years, I stopped working for someone else. It's been a successful business. What's this got to do with Mark's murder?"

Luke wondered the same thing.

"Can you remember any projects Gerry worked on in the late Seventies or early Eighties?" asked Gus.

"Gerry's firm had dozens of minor projects on the go back then. Their bread and butter work was in Marlborough Lane, of course."

Now we're getting to it, Gus thought.

"That's where Mark's flat was, am I right?"

Luke sensed that question unsettled Jenny. He wondered why. Those beautiful old houses converted into flats were very desirable.

"Marlborough Lane, yes," said Gus, "a mixture of old properties and new builds. I believe the old houses first converted into flats at the end of the Sixties."

"They didn't all get done at the same time," said Jenny, "and by the Eighties, buyers wanted new kitchens and bathrooms, a different styling. So Gerry's firm went backwards and forwards, upgrading those flats for years. That's what I meant by their bread and butter."

"Certain professionals in Gerry's line of work get options as part of their salary package. Is that how Gerry acquired the flat?"

"He had the option to buy one of the flats at cost. Gerry exercised that option and put the flat in my name when Mark was born in 1985. He was ecstatic about having a son. We had no trouble renting it out. Gerry and I argued over it eighteen years later after he walked out. As part of the divorce, the solicitors thrashed out a deal, and I became Mark's landlady when he moved in."

"Why didn't you tell us this last week?" asked Gus.

Jenny shrugged.

"I didn't think it was relevant."

"It *was* relevant, though, wasn't it? I kept asking myself how Mark afforded that BMW. You told me he didn't ask for money for it. What arrangement did you come to with Mark? Did he pay a peppercorn rent? Your business is successful. You didn't need the money. If things got tight, you could sell this place and downsize."

"It was legal and above board," said Jenny Malone,

"Mark paid me one pound per calendar month until he died."

"At least a thousand pounds below the going rate," said Luke.

"It was my property; I could do what I liked," said Jenny. "Once the police finished their investigations, I rented it to a couple. After that, it's never been empty."

"Did Patrick Boddington know you were Mark's landlady?" asked Gus.

"Of course he did," said Jenny, "they were close. We established that."

"Patrick omitted to tell us," said Gus, "and that suggests the two of you agreed to hide that knowledge from us."

"If you say so," said Jenny.

"If you're hiding something, we will discover it, Mrs Malone," said Gus.

Jenny Malone stared out of the window. Whatever she hid wouldn't see the light of day without a fight. Gus decided that it didn't relate to the murder case.

"What did you learn there, guv?" asked Luke when they returned to the car.

"Mark saved a fortune, regardless of how much lower rents might have been back in 2005. No wonder he could afford that car. We learned money wasn't the motivator for Mark when Emir Polat spoke to him at a show about the smuggled dogs. Something else attracted him to the enterprise. He loved dogs, so their welfare was all-important to him."

"Mark thought he could save the dogs, guv. Is that it? God, that was risky with people like Turgut and Demir involved."

"Get us into the city, Luke. Let's see whether Patrick Boddington will sing for his supper."

The walk from the car park to the Abbey Courtyard took a different route with Luke as his guide. Gus wondered how many narrow streets and alleyways there were in the city. The gallery door was open, and two American tourists appeared to be concluding a purchase. The smile on Patrick's face was so broad that Gus wondered whether they'd bought the place outright.

Gus and Luke waited while the corpulent Californian couple waddled from the gallery with their purchase. One beautifully wrapped oil painting. Gus spotted a gap on the wall. They'd paid eight hundred pounds for a portrait of the Abbey. He'd admired it last week when he was here, but not to the tune of eight hundred pounds.

"What did you forget to ask me?" asked Patrick, casting an appreciative eye over Luke. Gus noticed that Patrick wore the same suit as last week. The keffiyeh was a sandy yellow to match his spectacles.

"We wanted to clear up a couple of points," said Gus, "first, Mark's secret phone. You flicked through its contents. Is there any chance you noted the numbers?"

"I might have scribbled them down before I threw the phone away," replied Patrick, "where that note would be now, I struggle to think."

"Struggle harder," said Gus. "We can wait."

"Before you dash off," said Luke, "you told us Mark said he didn't know the driver of the grey BMW who banged on his window at the JET garage. Was that the truth?"

"That was what Mark said. Why would I lie about something like that?"

"In that case," said Gus, "the only way they could have handed Mark that phone was for Emir Polat to visit Bath."

"Is that the Emir Pompey from the contact list?" asked Patrick.

"Yes, his proper name was Emir Polat. Why?" asked Luke.

"There's a greengrocer behind Southgate Street whose family name is Polat."

"It's a common enough surname among Turkish Cypriots," said Gus, "he may be related to that family. So we have most of the pieces of the jigsaw now. Have you remembered where you put those numbers yet, Mr Boddington?"

"In my office. It might take a minute."

"DS Sherman can go with you. I'll keep an eye on the shop, sorry, gallery."

Luke and Patrick returned in less than a minute. Luke had both numbers that Mark used to contact the gang.

"We'll leave you now, Mr Boddington," said Gus. "One last thing, why did you omit to tell us Jenny Malone was the landlady responsible for refreshing the paintwork and finding new tenants for her late son's flat?"

Patrick Boddington shook his head.

"Jenny Malone asked me never to reveal the owner's name."

"Is that the best you can do?" asked Gus.

"You came here to ask about Mark's murder. I've answered your questions on that matter. Unfortunately, the other subject has nothing to do with his death. I can't help you, I'm afraid."

"I told Mrs Malone we would discover what she's hiding," said Gus.

"Well, when you do, you'll discover that it's nothing to do with me."

Patrick Boddington stood by the gallery door and waited for them to leave. Once outside the Courtyard, he locked the door and lowered the blind.

"Eight hundred pounds must be a good enough reason

to pack it in for the day," said Gus, "I bet he's calling Jenny Malone now. What d'you reckon?"

"It doesn't relate to the murder," said Luke. "I reckon she told HMRC she was only collecting a peppercorn rent on the Marlborough Lane property after declaring the earnings from 1985. When that young couple moved in three years ago, she never mentioned earning twelve hundred pounds monthly in rent. Do you think I'm on the right track?"

"Almost there, Luke," said Gus, "one more step."

"Patrick guessed that was why Jenny did not want her name revealed as the owner when the police came calling. So instead, she pays him a sweetener every month out of her ill-gotten gains. It fits with Patrick's claim that he only scrapes by on what he earns through the gallery."

"Is there an honest person left in this world, Luke? Everyone's at it," said Gus. "Time to get back to the office. Let's see what Lydia and Neil make of this."

Forty-five minutes later, Gus and Luke rode up to the first floor of the Old Police Station.

Lydia was in conversation on the phone. Neil Davis seemed eager to pass on information.

"Lydia started on that phone list, guv, so I spoke to Julian Drummond. He sounded an odd bloke."

"What did he have to say?"

"Well, because I needed him to put names to faces for me, I arranged to Skype him, and he's even odder when you see him in the flesh, isn't he?"

Gus had to agree.

"Drummond was at a dog show in East Sussex the first time the gang members appeared in October 2013. He remembers Polat talking to half a dozen dog owners and wondering what they wanted. I've passed the names to Lydia so she can follow up."

"Excellent idea," said Gus.

"Drummond said he'd done his usual thing at these shows, taking photographs at every opportunity. The big bloke, probably Mehmet Demir, came across and threatened him because he thought Drummond had taken photos of him. Then the smooth talker, Polat, came over and asked Drummond about his King Charles Spaniel. Did Drummond take his dogs to shows? Would he be interested in taking deliveries of the most popular breeds if he could get them at a bargain price? Drummond didn't like the look of the big guy and told the pair he wasn't interested."

"Sensible move," said Luke.

"Drummond heard from other owners that Polat reckoned he needed a valid customer address for the animals he brought in," said Neil.

"What about quarantine laws?" asked Luke. "The entire set-up should have sounded dodgy from the start."

"Go back, Neil," said Gus. "Did Julian Drummond catch either Polat or Demir in those photos?"

"Yes, guv," said Neil, "he's forwarding everything he has for us. They appeared at other shows, and Drummond believes they're in the background on several photos he took. He's also sending the list of owners and breeders that live along the route Malone drove that Saturday evening."

"Well done," said Gus, "We'll have positive confirmation it was the same gang. But, of course, it would help if Turgut appeared at least once."

Lydia got off the phone and showed Gus the comments she'd received from owners who agreed to participate.

"I've spoken to one lady from Godalming who's been

showing dogs for thirty years. Gillian Corden, no relation, told me she agreed at first to take Labrador puppies from the man who approached her. She felt so intimidated by his companion that she would have agreed to anything to get rid of them."

"How soon before she heard from them again?" asked Gus.

"The ugly brute delivered the phone to her kennels two weeks later. That was how Mrs Corden described him, guv."

"Does she still have the phone?" asked Gus. "How often did they call her? How many Labradors has she bought from them?"

"That's just it, guv. Someone called to tell Gillian the deliveries got delayed. She rang back, querying when things would run to schedule. Mrs Corden had her first delivery of six puppies in August 2014. Gillian asked for twelve, but Polat told her that was impossible."

"So, the first contact was the previous October," said Gus, "the phone arrived two weeks later. Mark's phone started receiving calls in February. Check whether that coincides with when Gillian Corden got activity on her phone. Ask how many deliveries she received and on which dates."

"I'll get back to her for more details, but it sounded like she had four deliveries in total. Each delivery produced fewer puppies than promised. Mrs Corden only paid for the number she received, which was a bonus."

"Was she happy with the condition of the dogs when they arrived?" asked Luke.

"The dogs were healthy and had the necessary paperwork," said Lydia, "the only thing she thought odd was the puppies looked older than the certification stated."

"I imagine Mrs Corden said nothing to the gang

because she got the puppies dirt cheap and always found willing buyers for cute puppies," said Gus.

"We need to dig deeper into this puppy trade, guv," said Neil, "do you want me to look?"

"Luke enlightened me last week on the lucrative trade in the exotic breeds, Neil. Take a close look at Portsmouth and see if there's more to this than meets the eye. Why bother setting up this network of dealers if Polat could only import two dozen Labrador puppies for Mrs Corden in twelve months? Even if Mark and the other owners Polat recruited took similar amounts of differing breeds, it's still peanuts."

"This has been a strange case from the outset, hasn't it, guv," said Lydia. "First, it got written off as road rage. Then, because the same weapon killed Mark Allison, there was a vague suggestion it might be another case of mistaken identity."

"Since your review at the weekend, guv," said Luke, "it's more likely Mark wanted to stop this puppy trade, and that's what got him killed."

"That's my fault," said Gus, "I got stuck in a loop around his blessed BMW. Now I can stand back and see the bigger picture; we can get this wrapped up over the next few days."

"If Neil and Lydia follow up on the suggestions you've just discussed, what shall I do, guv?" asked Luke.

"As soon as Drummond's package of photographs arrives, collect everything we have on Polat and his gang ready to transfer to Trefor Davies in Marlborough. They carried out the original investigation; they should make the arrests. Our role is ending. We'll trace the people Mark visited the night he died and take their statements; gather what we can from Mrs Corden and Portsmouth to add to our evidence, and Trefor Davies can make a case for the Crown Prosecution Service."

Wednesday, 13 June 2018

"ARE WE READY TO GO, GUV?" asked Neil

"Yes, Neil. Luke has called ahead to the two pet shop owners we need to interview. Our first stop is in Marlborough to speak with Tony Weston at Scruffs."

"Where do they get these names, guv?" asked Neil.

"Why might be a better question, Neil."

Neil drove them to Marlborough, and Tony Weston was alone in the shop when they entered.

"I'm Gus Freeman, a consultant with Wiltshire Police. My colleague DS Davis has a few questions. Is there someone who can look after the shop while we talk?"

"I'll give my daughter a shout," said Tony Weston, "she's supposed to be working this morning. I'm not sure if she's out of bed yet. It can be quiet on a half-day."

"We can wait, Sir," said Neil looking around the store. "Do you handle dogs and cats?"

"We do," said Tony, "I changed the name three years ago. Scruffs caters for any breed of dog or cat. We used to specialise in poodles, but that didn't work out."

"Kira! Can you come here, please?" he shouted.

Gus wondered whether Kira would get here before they'd finished the conversation. The pet owners of Marlborough seemed in no rush to gather on the pavement outside.

"Keep your hair on,"

Kira breezed into the shop from the upstairs accommodation.

"I need to talk to the police, Kira. Can you serve anyone if they come in?"

"I suppose so," said Kira, giving Neil a close inspection.

"We're interested in when you first met Emir Polat, Sir," said Neil.

"That rogue," said Tony. "He was the reason for the change of name. I met him at Crufts in 2014, and he persuaded me to take poodles from him. They were always late arriving. The documentation was dodgy, and we had complaints from the buyers."

"You hoped it was a way to make your business more profitable, I guess?" asked Gus.

"It gets harder and harder each year," said Tony.

"How well did you know Mark Malone?" asked Neil.

"We bumped into Mark at dog shows, and as a fellow pet shop owner, we had many of the same contacts. So I would have classed him as an acquaintance, not a friend."

"Mark came here in May 2015, didn't he?" asked Gus. "On the night he died."

"We live over the shop," said Tony Weston. "Mark knocked on the door after seven o'clock. He wanted me to go to the police with him. One dog he'd received was ill, and the vet who examined it said she found traces of drugs. She saved the animal's life, but it was touch and go."

"Did you agree to join Mark in exposing the criminal operation?" asked Gus.

"No chance," said Tony, "keep it down. I don't want Kira to hear this. The one they called Mehmet fancied her. Kira was fourteen then. Polat made it clear that if I stepped out of line, he'd hand her to Mehmet. I was glad when the total nightmare ended. They scared me to death."

"How long after Mark came here did the smuggling stop?" asked Neil.

"None of us received any more puppies after Mark Malone died."

"How long did Mark stop here that night?" asked Gus.

"Thirty minutes, no more," said Tony. "Mark drove away, and Polat arrived ten minutes later. That's when they threatened me. I realised they were on Mark's tail, but I couldn't get involved. Kira's our only child."

"So, you never spoke to the police after Mark's death?" asked Neil.

"I'm not proud of how I handled it," said Tony, "and none of the others would stand beside Mark and challenge the gang. The police said road rage was at the bottom of it. We wondered whether the other driver was Emir Polat. If Mark's death was because of the dogs, then, as they'd killed once, my wife convinced me we shouldn't risk getting involved."

"That's enough for now, Mr Weston," said Gus, "DI Davis from your local nick will get in touch if he needs more. Thank you for your co-operation."

"Can I go back upstairs now, Dad?" asked Kira.

Gus and Neil left Tony Weston and his Scruffs and returned to the car.

"Where to now, guv?" asked Neil.

"We're meeting a Caroline McCartney in Great Bedwyn. She thought All For Dogs gave the right amount of clue to what she offered. So drive on, Neil."

"Fifteen minutes, guv," said Neil as he pulled up outside the pet shop.

"Keep those timings in mind, Neil," said Gus. "They appear to stack up with Mark's phone records. Remember that Drummond and Mark swapped calls at eight and five past."

Caroline McCartney stood behind the counter of her shop. A timid woman with no sign of a ring. Gus thought they attended school simultaneously, separated by twenty-five miles of Salisbury Plain.

"You must be the police," she said, "I expect you want to talk about Mark Malone."

Neil Davis made the introductions and asked Miss McCartney what contact she had with Mark.

"Mark was a pleasant boy," she replied, "very well-spoken and always polite. He was eighteen when I first met him at a show. We would chat over a cup of tea every show we attended after that. I used to teach at the local school. Since I retired, money's been tight, you know. So that was what made this proposition so interesting, at first."

"When did they approach you?" asked Neil.

"At Paws In The Park in West Sussex," she replied, "the man was smartly dressed and handsome. I'm afraid I enjoyed the attention he paid me. I asked Mark whether he thought it a good idea, and Mark was keen, so I thought, why not?"

"Someone delivered a mobile phone, I assume?" asked Gus.

"Yes, within two weeks. That man was intimidating. I wasn't so sure then that I'd done the right thing. When I next got a call from Emir, he put my mind at rest and apologised for his colleague's brusque behaviour."

"We know the deliveries proved to be an issue," said Gus, "what happened the night Mark came here? Was that the first occasion he'd visited you?"

"Oh yes, although we spoke at the dog shows, I wouldn't

invite gentlemen to my home. It's next to the church. I carried on living there after Mother passed."

"What time did Mark arrive?" asked Neil.

"Around eight o'clock. Mark sat in his car for a minute or two, making a phone call, and then he walked up the garden path. I couldn't imagine what he wanted."

"He wanted you to help him," said Gus.

"He begged me to help him," said Caroline, "I couldn't believe what he told me. Someone drugged one of his dogs. How terrible. Mark thought there was something sinister going on. I wanted to believe him, but who would treat dogs that way? It was unbelievable. I didn't have any trouble with the puppies I received. They looked older than the paper-work said, but who knows these days? Children grow up before you know it, don't they?"

"Did Mark stay long?" asked Neil.

"He was such a kind boy," said Caroline. "I could tell he wanted to leave, but he saw I was lonely and scared of Emir and the others. Mark stayed with me while we had tea and a slice of lemon drizzle cake. He left a few minutes before nine."

"Did you hear from Emir Polat, or the others, after that?" asked Gus.

"No, thank goodness," said Caroline McCartney. "I was well out of it."

"What did you think when you heard Mark died later that night?" asked Gus.

"I was sad, of course, but it was the other driver, wasn't it? He got angry at Mark over something. I don't know what the world's coming to."

"Thank you for your time, Miss McCartney," said Neil, "we'll let you carry on with your day. You've been most helpful."

Gus followed Neil from All For Dogs and walked to the car.

"Are you in a rush?" he asked as Neil pulled away from the kerb.

"We got what we wanted, didn't we, guv?"

"I was hoping she'd offer us a cuppa and a slice of cake before we left."

"The timings match what we got from Mark's phone," said Neil. "We've got enough for DI Davies to arrest Polat, Demir and Turgut. I wonder where they are and what their next money-making wheeze was?"

"Let's return to the office, Neil," said Gus, "we can combine what we've gathered this morning with the work Lydia and Luke have done. I want Trefor Davies to have everything on his desk by ten o'clock in the morning."

Friday, 15 June 2018

"ANOTHER DAY, ANOTHER COLLAR, GUV," said Neil when he arrived at the Old Police Station office.

"A satisfactory outcome to a messy business, Neil," said Gus. "I'll only work a half-day today. I want to spend time with Bert Penman this afternoon. His family's funerals take place at eleven in the morning in Saskatchewan."

"Seven hours ahead, aren't we, guv?"

"Yes, Clemency Bentham's ready to do the early evening shift. She'll do the prayers and the comforting. I'll be there to give Bert something else to occupy his mind."

"I could do with therapy after this week," said Neil. "Why do you think the government thought it sensible to relax the strict pet travel laws six years ago?"

"It was to bring them in line with EU standards. So they scrapped the six-month quarantine for any dog entering the UK. Animals could arrive twenty-one days after a rabies vaccination."

"All designed to make free trade easier," said Neil, "and the move led to a surge of legal and illegal dogs coming into the country. Polat bought puppies in Eastern Europe, falsified their documents and sold them to buyers such as Gillian Corden, Tony Weston, and Caroline McCartney."

"Polat and his friends were evil, Neil," said Gus, "they cashed in on poor port security to smuggle in those puppies through Portsmouth. As for what happened next, well, it beggar's belief."

"It didn't take long for Trefor Davies to get cracking," said Neil. "they located Demir and Turgut within hours. One was in Belmarsh, and the other was on remand. Turgut faced lesser charges, but he'd pushed his luck for too long. The three-strikes law would have seen him get a much longer sentence. So, he talked."

"Yes, Neil, Trefor Davies couldn't stop him," said Gus. "Turgut described the complete set-up. The vet, a cousin of Polat's on this side of the Channel and the gangs involved in mainland Europe. It was a nice touch of Trefor's to let you accompany him to Portsmouth when they arrested Eleni Macrides. I'm pleased we found her. She was instrumental in achieving the gang's wishes."

"You've got to hand it to those gangs, guv. They know how to organise schemes to maximise profit. Turgut told DI Davies that a Bulgarian outfit set up the Eastern European end of the puppy trafficking route. The drugs came into Belgium from Columbia via Italy, and Polat's gang had his cousin on the payroll. Macrides crossed the Channel every month to get the dogs ready to travel. She operated on them to get as many drugs as possible around the dogs' organs."

"Macrides returned to Portsmouth and retrieved the drugs," said Gus. "After Mark Malone's death, the gang ceased the smuggling operation. However, the vet carried on working in Portsmouth, which pleased Trefor Davies because you could arrest her yesterday."

"Mehmet Demir is serving time for armed robbery," said Neil, "and he can kiss goodbye to walking out at the end of his sentence. Demir has two murder charges lined up to greet him."

"Only one gang member left to find," said Luke, "what have you heard since yesterday afternoon, guv?"

"DS Mercer called me at home this morning, Luke. The final piece of the jigsaw, Emir Polat," said Gus. "He returned to Cyprus in 2016, and Turgut added his whereabouts into the mix in return for a lighter sentence. Trefor Davies had a European arrest warrant served on Polat yesterday evening by the local police in Paphos. The paperwork and mobile phones he had at his apartment could prove invaluable. Police on the continent are already chasing the trafficking gangs in several countries and are hopeful of making early arrests. So it's been a busy and successful week."

"When is it not, guv?" said Lydia.

"Can we start wiping the whiteboards clean, guv," asked Luke, "ready for our next cold case?"

"We can remove the images and the words, Luke, but this case leaves a nasty taste in the mouth, doesn't it? At the outset, we thought Mark Malone died because he owed money to a crime gang or crossed them somehow. It turned out he was braver than any of the others contacted by Polat. He cooperated with them, hoping to learn enough to smash the evil trade they operated. They killed Mark and closed the smuggling operation. Even if it lasted only a year, it was a lucrative trade."

"I can't believe they used dogs like that," said Lydia.

"Even if you're not a dog lover, it was abhorrent," said Gus. "It's odd, though, isn't it? The gangs got the different elements of the business set up and working like clockwork. They sourced the puppies and transported them across Europe to Antwerp, stashed the drugs inside the animals and shipped them across the Channel to Portsmouth. All they needed to do was butcher the dogs and get the drugs out. Once they had the product, they didn't need them."

"That's gross, guv," said Lydia, "how could you even think of butchering the puppies?"

"Why baulk at killing the survivors? Polat went to the trouble of finding unsuspecting people who would take the puppies after they'd had a spell of healing. Hence the confusion in Gillian Corden's mind over the age of the puppies when she received them. Ask yourself, why the discrepancy in the quantities? Sometimes packages split in transit. Human drug mules have suffered that fate. Maybe the dogs got traumatised by the long journey and the initial surgery to insert the packages. We'll probably never know the scale of how many died en route. Polat and Macrides were comfortable with those losses. They still recovered the drugs."

"When do you think Mark Malone rumbled them, guv?" asked Neil.

"Three months before the first JET garage incident," said Gus.

"You've got me, guv. I don't recall seeing another JET garage incident in the murder file."

"It was never in the file, Neil. When Luke delivered the

first batch of evidence we'd gathered on Tuesday morning, Trefor Davies told him he couldn't believe the coincidence. One of his team was clearing out an old filing cabinet and found a loose folder that didn't relate to items nearby. Instead, it was a statement from a lady at the garage on a Sunday morning. A BMW with tinted windows and a black SUV parked beside one another. The driver in the BMW shouted at the men in the SUV. She was sure he mentioned a sick dog he had taken in a few days earlier. He'd rushed it to the vet. They told him it had ingested drugs, and they operated on the dog and saved its life."

"That was the night Mark went to the sex party on the other side of Salisbury," said Luke. "The black SUV stayed the night to follow Mark home."

"The pressure was building, and Mark realised what was going on. Polat thought he could get away with threats and intimidation. Mark wouldn't back off, so they silenced him. Trefor Davies has enough now to charge Mehmet Demir with Mark's murder. We keep doing that guy favours. He'll enjoy telling the Met he's found Mark Allison's killer into the bargain. That's another unsolved case filed away."

"Teamwork pays off every time," said Neil, "another case completed.

"Will there be a Crime Review Team party tonight?" asked Luke.

"Gus might be busy," said Lydia.

"I'll need a drink by nine o'clock," sighed Gus, "Waggon & Horses again?"

"Sounds good," said Lydia, "it will do Alex good to get out."

"I might persuade Melody to join me, guv," said Neil, "but no promises."

"We understand, Neil," said Luke.

"What was odd about Polat finding an outlet for his surviving puppies, guv?" asked Lydia.

"If Polat hadn't gone to the trouble of contacting Mark and the others, then Mark would have been alive today. The gang could still be smuggling drugs into the country inside puppies. He wasn't that heartless after all."

"It just goes to show that we're not the only nation of dog lovers, guv," said Luke, "and criminals can be as soft over them as we are."

"A schoolboy error," said Neil, "they were mad to do it, weren't they?"

"They were, Neil," said Gus, "please don't say what you were about to say.."

"Barking mad, guv?" said Neil.

"You couldn't resist it, could you? It's good to have you back, though."

Next in The Freeman Files series

vinci-books.com/creaturediscomforts

A cold case. A family above the law. One determined detective.

When gang leader Grant Burnside was killed by a sniper in 2014, the case went cold. Four years later, retired detective Gus Freeman is pulled back into the fold to navigate a labyrinth of secrets surrounding the impenetrable Burnside family.

Turn the page for a free preview…

Creature Discomforts: Chapter One

The Mercedes van drove out of the warehouse one hour later. Denver Drewett and Vic Hodge stayed behind to carry out the clean-up. Gary Burnside and his father had a delivery to make. The mortal remains of Howard Todd were on their way to a farm near Blunsdon. Grant took the A419 road towards Cricklade and turned off onto the minor road that led to the farm.

Thirty-five minutes later, they parked outside an outbuilding. It was a trip they had made frequently when someone stepped out of line, and an example made. Fergus McHugh's family had farmed here for three generations. Although pig farming had significantly contributed to the family income for many decades, Fergus accepted the inevitability of the need to diversify.

Grant Burnside had bumped into Fergus McHugh in a pub in Purton four years ago. He remembered the conversation very well. Grant had always lived in town, so his impression of pigs was false. He thought they were filthy animals, and Grant stood further along the bar from Fergus to avoid the stench. The farmer had told him pigs were the cleanest animals in the farmyard. They wallowed in mud to cool themselves because they didn't have sweat glands.

Grant asked Fergus how he felt about slaughtering a proportion of his stock every winter. The elderly farmer shrugged and replied that it was part of pig farming. But, because it was vital, his father had reduced the disposal of things with zero marketable value to a fine art. Fergus had adopted the same system when he inherited the farm after his father died.

Grant thought this disposal system sounded promising and bought Fergus another pint. He moved closer and invited Fergus to tell him more.

"Lye is a corrosive alkali found in household cleaners," the farmer told him. "Most people realise acids are caustic, but few realise that their chemical opposites can be just as destructive. Lye's toxicity at the highest can be super toxic."

"So, that's what you use then," asked Grant, "It works better than a lime-pit such as the ones you see in the films, does it?"

"Never believe what those filmmakers tell you," Fergus had said. "It takes less than seven drops in an oral dose, a mere taste, to be lethal to a seventy-kilogram human being. A single taste of lye causes third-degree burns on the mouth and the tube connecting the throat to the stomach. If a sufficiently large dose of lye gets swallowed, the alkali can cause perforations in the stomach, leading to death."

"I admit it sounds like a gruesome way of killing someone," Grant said, taking a swig of his pint. "But how do you persuade someone to drink the stuff? If they did, you've still got a body on your hands. How do a few drops of this lye stuff help to get rid of the bits of pig you've got left?"

Fergus McHugh explained the process.

"Under high heat and pressure, lye turns corrosive enough to disintegrate fat, bones, and skin. In three hours, my lye solution, heated to three hundred degrees Fahrenheit, dissolves an entire body into an oily brown liquid."

"Just say, for argument's sake, I had something I wanted to dispose of," Grant had asked. "Could you do it for the right price?"

Fergus McHugh had thought for a moment and then nodded.

"The equipment stands idle most of the time. If you see me right financially, I don't see a problem. After the process is over, I pour the oily liquid down the drain."

Grant decided to immediately change their method of disposing of bodies. Before that chance meeting in the pub, he, and his father before him, buried any corpses in nearby woods or dumped them in sewers or the river. That method was risky. Dead bodies could be discovered and the evidence they contained used against them. Fergus McHugh's operation offered a perfect solution.

Grant had called yesterday to tell Fergus McHugh that a van would arrive this morning. Fergus's job was to make sure he had enough stock whenever someone from the Burnside gang delivered a package to be able to carry out his side of the bargain.

Grant and his son entered the outbuilding and loaded Todd's remains into the large steel container in the centre of the room. Grant placed an envelope filled with the cash payment on a nearby table.

As they drove out of the yard, Grant knew Fergus would appear from inside the farmhouse. Once inside the outbuilding, the elderly farmer put on protective gloves and a gas mask. He then boiled the package in the lye solution for eight hours until only the teeth, and the nails remained.

Fergus destroyed those last pieces of evidence by burning them with petrol in a wood near the farm boundary.

Fergus and Grant hadn't met in person since that night four years earlier. The occasional phone call was the only link between them. Nobody questioned why an unmarked van appeared in the farmyard to make a delivery. Why should they?

"That was money well spent," said Grant as they returned to the Cheney Manor Industrial Estate to collect Denver and Vic, the clean-up crew,

"Sly Todd has disappeared for good," said Gary. "There's no danger of us getting linked to anything. We'll do what we always do, make sure the right people know why he's not around. It will send a clear message not to cross us."

"What are you doing later?" asked Grant, "this work has made me hungry. Once we've dropped off your gophers, why don't we collect the girls and go for a Sunday lunch?"

Gary wasn't sure his stomach was stable enough to tuck into a roast dinner after this morning's events. But he knew his father didn't want to hear that, so he called Kirstin and told her to get ready.

"Do you want me to call Maggie?" asked Kirstin, "to warn her Grant will expect her to be ready to jump to it as soon as he reaches home?"

"Good idea," said Gary, "forewarned is forearmed. I'll see you within the hour. I need to shower and change before we go out."

Denver and Vic were still inside the warehouse unit when Grant backed the Mercedes van up to the roller door.

Gary went inside to check on their progress. He needn't have worried. The heavy-duty plastic sheeting had been hosed down and stacked away in the corner. The unit floor bore no visual evidence of what had occurred two hours earlier.

"Did you clean the tools, too?" he asked.

Denver Drewett nodded.

"They're locked in the cabinet, ready for use whenever needed," he replied.

"Come on then," said Gary. "We'll drop you two home, and then we can enjoy what's left of Sunday."

As the three men walked towards the exit, they heard a crack.

"What the heck was that?" asked Vic.

"It sounded like a car backfiring," said Denver.

Gary thought it sounded more like a gunshot, but it couldn't be, not in the middle of nowhere.

Once they were outside, Denver and Vic climbed into the back of the van, and Gary locked the unit door. He looked around the various industrial units, but nobody was working, and no other vehicles were in sight.

"What was that loud bang just now, Dad?" Gary asked as he prepared to swing himself into the passenger seat of the truck's cab.

The neat hole in the windscreen caught his attention first, and when he turned his head to the right, Gary saw what remained of his dead father's face.

Gary fell back out of the cab, collapsed to his knees and threw up.

Denver Drewett and Vic Hodge banged on the sides in the back of the truck, wanting to know what had happened. When he recovered, Gary let them out.

"Who would have wanted to shoot Grant?" asked Drewett.

Vic Hodge didn't say a word. He knew Denver was brighter than him. But be fair. Even Vic knew there was a list as long as your arm of people who wanted Grant Burnside dead.

Vic thought the question should be—who dared to do it? There wouldn't be many names on *that* list.

"What do you want us to do, Gary?" he asked.

"We can't leave him there," said Denver.

"Just shut it for a minute, will you?" yelled Gary, "I need to think."

Gary realised there was no way to cover this up. He had to call the police, even if it was the last thing he wanted to do.

Gary looked at the windscreen again. Where had the shot come from? Dad wouldn't have sat there and let a gunman walk up to the van and open fire. It had to be a rifle with a large calibre bullet to make that mess. Could there have been a sniper lying on the roof of one of the other warehouse units? Any gunman would be long gone by now. How the heck did they know Grant was going to be here this morning? It was a Sunday, and Dad never worked on a Sunday. Gary was desperately trying to think who could have fired the shot that ended his father's life.

"Are we certain that everything connecting us to Howard Todd has gone from inside that warehouse?" he asked.

"Forensics might find something, Gary," said Denver. "You need to get hold of Iverson. He'll know what to do."

Gary made the call, and Patrick Iverson drove into the yard twenty minutes later. He'd been the Burnside family solicitor for half a century. What he didn't know about the family's crooked dealings and punishment beatings wasn't worth knowing.

His legal representation didn't come cheap, but Grant's father, George, had argued that if Iverson kept him out of prison, it was worth every penny. So Iverson was suited and booted, as always, and parked his Jaguar far away from the Mercedes.

Vic Hodge wondered whether he ever went out without wearing a suit and tie.

"What happened?" asked Iverson, approaching the van but keeping his distance from the cab.

"Dad and I had business to attend to," said Gary. "We visited here earlier with these two and carried out the first phase. Then we drove out Blunsdon way, finished our business, and returned. I went inside to collect Vic and Denver, and someone shot Dad."

"Don't tell me what the business was," said Iverson. "I don't want to know. Is there anything incriminating in the van?"

"I'll check the cab," said Gary, swallowing hard. "I don't think Dad had a weapon of any kind. There might be blood on the floor in the back."

Patrick Iverson shuddered.

"What about inside the warehouse?"

"We cleaned it well, Mr Iverson," said Vic Hodge.

"Yeah, it's clean, but it might not be good enough to fool forensics," added Denver Drewett.

"That's okay," said Iverson, "check the van's rear compartment. If you have bleach available, spread it liberally on any affected areas. I'll think up a plausible explanation. As for the unit, the police will need to get a search warrant. There's nothing to suggest it's connected to the killing. If nobody saw you earlier, you can say the shooting occurred as soon as you arrived. You didn't have time to work inside before rushing outside to help Grant. I know what you want to do, Gary, but please don't rush to the other units searching for clues. Leave that to the police. We need to act fast. We can't delay notifying the authorities for much longer."

Gary checked the glove compartment and the floor of the cab. As he had thought, there weren't any hidden weapons. The paperwork for the vehicle was in order—nothing to fear there. Vic and Denver checked inside the van. Because they'd done a grand job of wrapping Howard Todd's body parts, there were only a few stains that needed a quick scrub with bleach from the warehouse unit toilet. Patrick Iverson took a quick look.

"Okay, Gary, make the call," he said. "When they ask what time I arrived, tell them you rang me immediately after you made the emergency call, and I was driving towards the Manor."

Iverson turned to the others and said, "Leave as much talking to me as possible, do you understand?"

Denver and Vic nodded.

Ten minutes later, the four men heard sirens in the distance.

Grab your copy...
vinci-books.com/creaturediscomforts

About the Author

Ted Tayler is the international bestselling indie author of The Freeman Files and The Phoenix series. Ted lives in the English west country, where his stories are based. He was born in 1945 and has been married to Lynne since 1971. They have three children and four grandchildren.

His thought-provoking mysteries appeal to readers of Sally Rigby, Joy Ellis, Pauline Rowson, and Faith Martin. His action-packed thrillers are a must for fans of Mark Dawson and J. C. Ryan.

Gus Freeman's cold case investigations are carried out with reasoned deduction rather than bursts of frantic action. In each of the twenty-four books, unsolved murder is accompanied by romance, humor, and country life. The core message in the twelve Phoenix novels is that criminals should pay for their crimes. Unfortunately, the current system fails to deliver the correct punishment, so Phoenix helps redress the balance.

Acknowledgments

The love and support of my family; without them, this would have been impossible.

www.ingramcontent.com/pod-product-compliance
Lightning Source LLC
Chambersburg PA
CBHW011427010726
47494CB00011B/2531